Dawlish was on holiday at Bournemouth, enjoying himself in his own way – relaxing on the tennis courts. Relaxing, indeed, to such good effect that he won the All-Comers Tournament. In the resultant publicity he caught up with an old friend from wartime days, Colonel Reginald Osgood. It was after a celebration dinner at Ossy's house that Dawlish and his wife first heard the pure, high sound of a trumpet . . . And it was the trumpet motif which was to plague Dawlish all through the nightmare days which followed . . .

## Also by John Creasey

and published by Corgi Books

John Creasey as Gordon Ashe

# A Blast of Trumpets

**CORGI BOOKS**
A DIVISION OF TRANSWORLD PUBLISHERS LTD

# A BLAST OF TRUMPETS

A CORGI BOOK 0 552 10253 9

Originally published in Great Britain by
John Long Limited

PRINTING HISTORY
John Long edition published 1975
Corgi edition published 1976

This book is set in Monotype Times

Corgi Books are published by
Transworld Publishers Ltd.,
Century House, 61–63 Uxbridge Road,
Ealing, London W5 5SA
Made and printed in Great Britain by
Cox & Wyman Ltd., London, Reading and Fakenham

# CONTENTS

## CHAPTER ONE

# THE REFUSAL

'WHY don't you want to go?' asked Polkov. 'Isn't the money good enough?'

'Oh, the money's wonderful.' The blue eyes of young Jim Ryall lit up with unfeigned enthusiasm.

'Then why on earth turn it down?' Polkov demanded.

'Well . . .' Ryall hesitated. 'I suppose it's mostly because I'm English, but it's partly that – oh, well, I'm happy here. I don't want to leave.'

'Or do you mean your wife won't let you?' demanded Polkov.

It was immediately obvious that he had said the wrong thing; Ryall's eyes became cold, and all enthusiasm died. His voice changed, and so did his expression as he said:

'I'm not coming.'

'Now, Jim—'

'And don't "now, Jim" me,' Ryall said acidly. 'I am not coming.'

He turned away from the other and stalked across the hotel room which Polkov had hired for a number of interviews. The carpet was a thick, dark red. The walls were pale-coloured between mathematically hung pictures depicting scenes of the English civil war. Each scene was vivid; whether of the battlefield, or the House of Commons, or the King's Palace, or of one of the cathedrals savaged by Cromwell. This was a small town in the English Midlands. Once, a vicious battle had been fought here, on ground across the highway from the main doors of the hotel.

The town was Wilbury, the hotel the Royal Wilbury Arms.

Jim Ryall felt the sharp pleasure of a south-west wind which had swept across the distant fields, through streets where most of the cottages were oak-beamed and thatched, and across the ruins of the castle where that last desperate battle had been fought.

It was September; and in the air was the sweet scent of new-mown hay.

He moved towards the car park at one side of the Royal Wilbury Arms, and came in sight of the distant factory where he worked. The factory of glass, some called it; or the Glasshouse if you were an old soldier. It was of two storeys and the walls were made of a glass-like ceramic, tough and weather-resistant as any stone or brick, whatever its decriers might say. Beyond it were the experimental bays and sheds, and the big hangars; and beyond these again, the measuring rooms and the underground research establishment where he, James Ryall, worked.

An aircraft was coming in to land – yet there was little sound.

He could see it clearly: a twin-jet Astic, a fairly old model fitted recently with new engines: and here it came, with scarcely a sound. As if to heighten the effect of this near-silence another aircraft, probably heading for the Birmingham airfield, came into sight, and soon began to roar. It passed, as the Astic came low, climbed, flew a few miles out and then came back.

It sank out of sight beyond the main building, and no doubt touched down; but there was no great sound of the engines reversing; from where he stood, no noise at all.

Ryall was smiling again, wholly at peace, for he had just seen and heard a kind of miracle, which he himself had helped to make.

'Wonderful,' Polkov said quietly into his ear. 'How long did it take you and your team?'

'Six years.'

'At least four too many,' Polkov stated, and this time Ryall turned round sharply, contentment broken, and demanded:

'What do you mean?'

'You took six years instead of two to find the answer to the question of jet-noise because you hadn't enough money to work fast.'

'Fast work isn't always the best.'

'But it can be, Jim, you know that as well as I do. You know, too, that you and your team were frustrated nearly

8

out of your wits by lack of money. You had to wait months, sometimes, for a small piece of equipment which was holding up all the rest of the work. Can you deny it?'

'Maybe not, but the fact remains that we've beaten the rest of the world to it,' Ryall declared, and there was a glow in his eyes: of personal satisfaction and pride that he and his team of English experts had solved one of the aircraft industry's greatest problems.

'Jim,' said Polkov, 'you are not small-minded.'

'What do you mean by that?'

'You wouldn't make the rest of the world wait four years simply to say we were first.'

'We,' wondered Ryall, although not very deeply. Was Polkov English? For how many generations? Three or four could make him English in spirit as well as in law, but one might not be enough. He *looked* English. On the dark side, perhaps, but with clear hazel-brown eyes and curly, greying hair and the weatherbeaten face one found in countrymen.

'The truth is, that this company hasn't enough capital – any more than Rolls-Royce had enough capital when they ran into trouble. Very few individual groups have: you need a consortium and a bottomless well of money to be able to keep big projects going. You have one of the finest brains in aeronautics; you could easily waste it here.'

'And overcoming jet-engine noises?' Ryall scoffed.

'That isn't the only thing you have on the boards,' said Polkov. 'There's no end to new possibilities, new inventions, new methods. Give yourself a chance, Jim, and do right by aeronautics.' When Ryall didn't answer, Polkov went on: 'I shouldn't have made that crack about your wife just now. I'm sorry.'

Ryall waved a hand. 'Forget it.'

'If you'll reconsider—'

'No,' interrupted Ryall, 'I will not reconsider. It is not simply that I want this country to get some credit for what it's doing.' He was facing the other man very squarely and speaking with great deliberation. 'It is not simply because I don't want to uproot my wife and family. It's just . . .' He hesitated, frowned, and finally went on wonderingly: 'I just don't feel that it would be right.'

After a long pause, Polkov said: 'Not even at twice the sum offered?'

'Not at any price,' Ryall replied, and then he gave a short, mirthless laugh. 'But I must say you and your principals really want me, if you'd pay as much as twenty thousand pounds a year plus a house and all travel expenses.'

'Oh, yes,' Polkov said. 'We want you. We want all—'

He broke off abruptly, staring at Ryall as if to judge whether the other had seen the significance of the 'all' and guessed how he had been going to finish: '*all* the best brains in aeronautics.' But Ryall seemed not to have noticed; it was almost as if the offer to double his salary was dazzling him; and that he would soon change his mind.

But he did not.

Polkov drew the telephone nearer, and lifted the receiver. He dialled a London number and was answered very quickly by a woman with a voice which carried a slight European accent.

'This is Zemcon.'

'This is Polkov,' Polkov said.

'You will wait a moment, please.'

Polkov waited, as he often had.

The peculiar fact about his association with Zemcon was that he did not know where its offices were, had never visited them, had never seen anyone who worked for them, as far as he knew. He had spoken to this woman and to others with noticeably accented voices, but only to one man, whose voice was unmistakably British.

As he waited he kept thinking of Jim Ryall.

Ryall was cycling along towards the thatched cottage which he owned. It was set at the end of a narrow lane where there were other, similar cottages, all backed by a line of fine trees. As the cottage came into view the front door opened and Janet, his two-year-old daughter, came running. She was as golden-haired as Anne, his wife, who now appeared in the open door-way, smiling happily, watching as Jim sprang from his bicycle, rested it against a post, then held out his arms to the child.

Soon, he sat her on the saddle and wheeled her round to the back of the house, as happy and delighted as the child herself.

Returning, Janet scampering by his side, he put one arm

round his wife's waist, held her close, and kissed her.

'I love you.'

'I love *you*.'

'How would you like to leave this medieval battleground and go to a brave new world?'

'I'd hate it.'

'At double the money?'

She strained away from him, to look into his eyes. 'Did they really double the offer?'

'Yes, my sweetheart, they did.'

'What did you do?'

'I said no.'

She strained still further away, and drew her brows together in concentration. Janet had gone chasing birds, a daily gay futility, and they were alone in the kitchen with the shadows of beech trees darkening the window.

'Really want to turn it down, darling?'

'I do.'

'*Not* just because of me?'

'Good gracious me! Why should I consider you in such a highly personal issue?' He kissed her again, and this time she relaxed completely against him, until Anne came up busily, a pigeon feather in her hand, and Jim drew away. 'I've enough and to spare for you and Janet and two or three more if it pleases you. I'd hate to move away.'

'I don't think you would hate it any more than I would,' Anne answered him. 'Goodness, it's a quarter past one! You won't have time to gulp a thing down and I've apple pie for dessert!'

At last Polkov's period of waiting ended, and the very English voice sounded in his ear in the familiar conversational tone.

'What is it, Polkov?'

'I've just seen Ryall.'

'Well?'

'He won't come.'

'Did you double the offer?'

'Yes – and it didn't have the slightest effect on him. He—' Polkov broke off.

'Go on.'

'He simply wouldn't budge, sir. I – I think I made a slip.'

'Indeed? What kind of slip?' There was an edge to the cultured voice.

'He made some crack about being very badly wanted, and I said we wanted all—'

'*All* aeronautical research workers? You must have taken leave of your senses!'

'It wasn't as bad as that,' said Polkov. 'I stopped at "all" and I don't think he read any significance in it, but he might do if he starts pondering. And you've always made a point of wanting to know anything which could give anyone ideas. I shouldn't have said "all". I'm sorry.'

There was a long pause before the Englishman spoke again.

'That's a handsome apology and a frank admission. Neither will do you any harm. Was Ryall the last one in Wilbury?'

'Yes, sir.'

'The other four have signed contracts?'

'Yes – signed and sealed and the first payment made. There's nothing to worry about with them. Not that I seriously think there's anything to worry about with Ryall, sir.'

'I am quite sure there won't be,' the Englishman said, in a tone which allowed no doubt at all.


The moon shone over a sleeping countryside.

Only the sounds of the fields and the hedgerows murmured in the silence; that and the clucking of a chicken farm over the brow of a hill from the Ryalls' cottage.

They kept no dog; so no dog barked when the man appeared, on foot, from among the beech trees. He walked around the cottage, seeing the four upstair windows open; none was open downstairs. He went to the back door and, using a tool with skill and stealth, forced the lock.

Inside the cottage, he took a tin of powder from his pocket, then looked at the gas stove; the pilot light was on. He sprayed first the kitchen, then the staircase, and then placed the tin on the gas stove close to the lighted pilot. He screwed the top on tightly before leaving the way he had come.

He walked straight to the beech trees, and disappeared.

Upstairs the Ryalls and their child lay sleeping. None of

12

them stirred. The vapour crept upstairs and deepened their sleep; they were not even aware of the fire when it began with a sharp explosion.

As they slept they died.

The coroner returned a verdict of death by accident and added some caustic remarks about aerosol sprays which, if heated, would cause gases noxious enough to be lethal.

Only one man in the coroner's court had any reservations. He was the chief security officer at the Glasshouse, a middle-aged man with the unusual name of Pence.

CHAPTER TWO

## PRESENTING MR. DAWLISH

'FIFTEEN-LOVE,' the umpire called.

'Go on, Pat, go on,' breathed Felicity Dawlish, as her husband caught a ball tossed to him by a ball boy and went back to serve again. Five hundred people watched, and four hundred of them were praying for the other man, the local hero, to win. Only a few had much enthusiasm for the big stranger.

Very few knew more than his name: Patrick Dawlish.

Among those few were a dozen or so policemen, each one of them tense in his support; for they knew who he was. It was almost a miracle in this two-day All-Comers Tournament at Bournemouth that Dawlish had not been more widely identified, for he was one of Britain's top policemen.

Now he tossed the ball up; struck; and *swisssh* the service went, not an inch above the net and in the far corner of the local hero's court.

'Thirty-love.'

There was a ripple of applause, so much more than a ripple in one corner that Felicity looked round to see where the support was coming from. Dawlish tossed the ball up again.

13

*Swisssh* it went, into the net.

'Fault.'

There was a kind of hiss about the ground, an indication of tension.

*Up – thwack – swisssh.*

'Forty-love. Match point to the challenger.'

'Pat, just one more, just one,' breathed Felicity.

Others called out, and received a stern rebuke.

'Silence, please.'

Up – thwack – *swisssh.*

A line judge called: 'Fault.'

Dawlish stretched to his full six feet four, and then on to his toes to become a gigantic six foot seven. He tossed the ball, then struck it squarely, although with no great force. It sailed over the net and dropped a yard in front of the local hero, who touched it with the edge of his racquet and sent it into the net.

'Game, set and match to . . .'

No doubt the umpire said 'The Challenger' but the words were drowned in a roar from the police group and cheers from the uniformed policemen who so seldom showed which side they favoured. The local hero came up to the net.

'Congrats,' he said, warmly. 'I'm glad you didn't strike your form until the last set or I wouldn't have scored a point.'

'Very generous,' Dawlish said. 'Thank you.' Then he saw Felicity hurrying, and sensed her delight.

'Pat, you were magnificent!'

'Look who I had rooting for me,' Dawlish said, laughing. Felicity laughed too. She was a tall woman, good-looking without being beautiful in anything but her quite lovely green-grey eyes.

'Yes,' she said. 'Who were they?'

'Eh?' ejaculated Dawlish. 'I meant you.'

'There was a group up there,' She turned to look at the terrace seats which were now empty. 'Oh, they've gone.'

'I didn't hear them,' Dawlish said.

'I haven't seen you concentrate on a game like that for years,' said Felicity. 'Why did you?'

'I wanted the perfect finale to a perfect week,' he said. 'You didn't think I would actually take a full week off, did you?'

14

'No,' Felicity admitted. 'I—'

Then photographers and officials arrived and the finalists and semi- and quarter-finalists, in fact all who had fought that day, were photographed and re-photographed, while Dawlish was presented with a bronze trophy and a cheque for £250. There, too, was the mayor of Bournemouth, youthful and bright-eyed, to receive a cheque for £1,000 for his special mayoral charity; with him was his dark-haired, olive-skinned wife and with them a grey-haired man who walked with a pronounced limp.

The chairman of the Bournemouth Tennis Club was introducing them, and he came soon to the grey-haired man.

'Colonel Osgood, allow me to present Mr. Patrick Dawlish, the winner as you know. Mr. Dawlish, Colonel Osgood is the president of the Bournemouth and District Rehabilitation Centre and Workshops for the Disabled and . . .'

'Ossy!' gasped Dawlish.

'By all that's holy – Patrick Dawlish!'

Suddenly the two men were shaking hands as if there was no one else in the world; and Felicity, watching the expression on her husband's face, knew that for him this was a moment of sheer pleasure. Even the chairman and the mayor realized this, and turned to others.

'You mean you didn't recognize me on the court!' Dawlish still gripped the other's hand.

'I'm so short-sighted these days. But, Pat, what a wonderful chance. What are you doing here? Are you alone? Is your wife . . . ?' Dawlish drew Felicity in front of him and he was taking her hand and looking at her searchingly. 'So you're the Felicity I used to hear so much about . . .'

'Sweetheart, Colonel Osgood was with me on the first jump I ever made behind the German lines . . .'

'And I jumped so badly I broke my leg!'

'And hid up in some trees rather than crawl out for help from the enemy.'

'You must have been the first parachutist to get away from France . . .'

'I'll never forget . . .'

At last Felicity persuaded them to interrupt the reunion and they went back to the official party, duly apologetic. Dawlish found that he still held the cheque in his hand. He looked at the mayor with his larger cheque, and asked: 'Do

15

you have a pen, sir?' The mayor handed him a gold ball-point and Dawlish placed the cheque on Felicity's stiff linen bag, endorsed it and handed it to the mayor with the pen. 'May I add this?'

'My dear sir! You are very . . .'

Talk and chatter, laughter and questions, tea in a huge and airy room, where photographers went from table to table. One of them came towards Dawlish accompanied by a girl who held a stub of pencil and a dog-eared notebook in her hand. She looked at him with very earnest brown eyes.

'You are *the* Mr. Dawlish, aren't you? The Assistant Commissioner at Scotland Yard?'

'Be sure my sins . . .' said Dawlish, with pretended lugubriousness. 'If you have to write it down, Deputy Assistant Commissioner—'

'For international crime?'

'You could say that.'

'You really *did* launch the Crime Haters, didn't you?'

'He did indeed,' said Felicity, 'but he hates to admit it. Don't be so mock-modest, Pat.' They were alone but for the girl and the photographer, who stood by, his camera clicking at odd times and from odd angles. 'Won't you sit down?' Felicity asked the girl.

'I'd love to.' The girl's gaze was still fixed on Dawlish; she seemed to be mesmerized by him. 'I couldn't believe it was you in spite of the name, but when I saw nearly every C.I.D. man in Bournemouth cheering you on, I knew you must be you. I'm Sue Day, from the *Echo*, by the way. Would you mind if Southern Television comes and takes a few shots?'

'If they really want to,' Dawlish conceded.

'You should have heard them when I told them who you were.'

Slightly embarrassed by so much adulation Dawlish said brightly: 'How much do you know about the Crime Haters?'

'Everything I can find out,' Sue Day replied. 'I know it's really an International Police Conference, that you've been on the ruling body for years, that you hold conferences in different countries, very often, that you have an official headquarters in Golana, Africa – don't you find that difficult?' she asked in an aside.

'Not really, in these days of teleprint and telepictures and instant communication,' Dawlish answered. 'I won't pretend

16

it's as convenient as if it were in London or New York but on the whole it works. The world's changing shape, you know.'

'May I quote you?'

'I won't say a word that shouldn't be quoted.'

'Wonderful!' The brown eyes glowed, and Sue turned them towards Felicity. 'He's just as natural as everyone's told me!'

'Everyone?' asked Felicity.

'I've lots of friends and acquaintances in the police force here,' Sue explained. 'And some London reporters come down for big cases, and they all say the same – that within two minutes you feel as if you've known him for days! You *do* only deal with international crime, don't you?'

'Or crime which might cross frontiers,' Dawlish told her. 'There can be a major crime in London at noon and the perpetrators can be in America before nightfall and any-where in the world within twenty-four hours. What we are trying to do is keep pace with crime.'

'Are you succeeding?' asked Sue Day, with sweet inno-cence of deep duplicity.

'Pretty well, I think,' said Dawlish. 'For a few years, before we were organized, the criminals had it largely their own way. It's not so easy for them now.'

'What exactly *do* you do?' asked Sue.

'Tell me what you know already,' Dawlish urged.

'Well . . .' She paused, but it was to collect her thoughts, not in hesitation. 'There are delegates from every police force in the world, from many big cities as well as national police forces – Chicago, New York and Los Angeles, for instance, and the F.B.I. Then Sydney and Melbourne have delegates, and—'

'You'll do,' Dawlish interrupted, but did not stop the flow.

'And each force that has a delegate has a department which specializes in crime with international repercussions – oh, and they all have expert linguists and usually officers who have travelled widely. *Is* that right?'

'You have most certainly done your homework,' Dawlish assured her.

The girl flushed with pleasure, and in the pause which followed a member of the club brought tea and sandwiches.

As they ate and drank a young man with a bald head came bearing down on them carrying a camera. On its side were the words: *Southern TV*. Hovering were two men, fixing a tripod.

'All this because I can hit a little ball,' remarked Dawlish. 'What would happen if we found an international smuggling ring in Bournemouth?'

'Oh, that wouldn't be half so important,' said Sue.

Dawlish's eyebrows rose. 'You can't be serious.'

'Oh, but I can. You've won something peculiar to Bournemouth. But—' She stopped short while cameras were levelled at him. Then: 'You haven't, have you?'

'Haven't what?'

'Found a smuggling ring here?'

Dawlish was surprised into a laugh.

'Not yet,' he assured her.

'*Is* it just a pleasure visit?' Sue demanded.

'A whole week's holiday which finishes tonight. Yes, ma'am.'

'Oh,' said Sue. 'That's a pity. Hallo, Tim,' she went on to the cameraman. 'Don't let me hold you up.'

'Bless your little cotton socks! Mr. Dawlish, I wonder if . . .?'

He asked a few questions while another, younger, man operated the camera. The B.B.C. TV followed. People hovered to listen, some to ask for autographs. Colonel Osgood sent a written message:

> My home (address over) seven-fifteen for seven-thirty, no need to dress, dinner with my wife and family who don't really believe in you. R.O.

The messenger vanished before Dawlish could send a note of thanks.

It was then half past five, there would be too little time to get back to their rented cottage and return here for dinner, but Felicity was wearing a suit which would serve well enough, and Dawlish flannels and a lightweight jacket. The obvious thing was to go to a hotel and freshen up, and the Royal Bath was not far away. Sue vanished, the crowd thinned, and the Dawlishes left with a minimum of fuss.

A policeman approached them.

18

'Good evening, Mr. Assistant Commissioner. Superintendent Moss would be very glad to have you and Mrs. Dawlish for drinks, sir, before you go on to Colonel Osgood. He's put a car at your disposal, sir, and asked me to say there are all facilities at headquarters. He would be here himself but he was called away on an urgent matter. And there's a man waiting to see you, sir, your people in London sent him down here.'

'Oh,' said Dawlish. He eyed the man steadily for a second or two. 'Do you have a walkie-talkie?'

'Certainly, sir.' The man produced a tiny transistor. 'Can I help you?'

'I'd like to talk to your headquarters,' Dawlish said, with a pleasant smile. 'No offence, Constable, but I have been fooled by phoney policemen before now.'

The man stared – and then laughed with genuine amusement.

A moment later Dawlish was talking to the Control Room in the local headquarters: all doubts set at rest, he and Felicity made their way to the waiting police car.

## CHAPTER THREE

## PENCE

'THIS is really a new station and we're very proud of it. If you have time tomorrow we'd be delighted to show you round.' Superintendent Moss was obviously eager that they should have time. He was a suntanned man in the middle forties, with very bright eyes and a precise manner: it was clear that he was an organizer. They were in his office with several other senior officers. A young woman in a cap and apron was pouring out drinks. 'You should have seen our chaps here when they heard you'd won. It's a good job we didn't have a lot of emergencies,' he added. 'For two hours this afternoon nearly every C.I.D. man in the force was out on some mysterious special investigation.'

'Haven't seen better at Wimbledon,' another man remarked.

'Blind luck,' demurred Dawlish.

'Not at all. Damned good tennis,' an elderly man declared.

They had been here for half an hour, and it was now nearly half past six. Moss assured them he would have them at Osgood's house on the West Cliff at the stroke of seven-fifteen; it was no more than a ten-minute run.

'You'll want to speak to the man your people sent down, won't you?' Moss added. 'I asked him to be here at a quarter to seven.'

'Yes,' Dawlish replied. 'Yes, of course. Is there an office where we can talk?'

'All laid on,' Moss assured him, and led the way out of the room.

Dawlish was not looking forward to the interview.

He was puzzled, because no one from his London office had warned him that any messenger was coming to see him here – but they must surely have sent him, for no one else knew where he was; officially he was in the New Forest. In any case, he felt in a completely relaxed mood, more so than for a long time. In one way that was why he had entered the tournament; it meant concentrating his physical as much as his nervous energy on something other than work.

And it had been just the climax he and Felicity had needed.

He could not recall how long ago it was since they had taken a week off together, free from interruption; goodness alone knew how long it would be before the next complete break.

And the final, unbelievable pleasure was the reunion with Osgood. He would hate to have it spoilt. And this mysterious man 'sent' to him might well take the edge off the evening. He had been tempted to tell the man to wait until morning, but had not been able to; and here he was, aware of Felicity's gaze on him as he went out with Moss. A youthful chief inspector was obviously greatly taken by her.

Moss gave a perfunctory tap on a door and opened it.

A man, seated rather uncomfortably, stood up.

Dawlish knew him at once; hesitated only for a moment, and then placed him. He was a stolid rock of a man, square-shouldered, square-jawed, flat-nosed, with deep-set eyes.

His hair was nearer white than grey and cut close to his head: it was not far from a prison cut. He had a long upper lip and a thin mouth, and appeared to be a very tough customer indeed.

'Good evening,' he said.

'You're Pence, aren't you? Chief Inspector Pence?' Dawlish said, and for good measure added: 'Hugo Pence.'

'Nice of you to remember, sir – but it's ex-chief inspector now. I retired three years ago and took up a private security post.' Pence had a hard voice, penetrating but not loud. The lines at his eyes seemed chiselled there, and the eyes themselves had a tired look. 'I'm sorry to worry you when you're on leave, but – well, I'm a very worried man, sir.'

'And you think I can help?'

'I'd go further than that and say you're the only one who can. Probably the only one who will listen, sir.'

Dawlish had no doubt that this man was deeply worried and that he would not have come here except as a last resort. The resentment and exasperation faded; the policeman in Dawlish – who for so many active years had not been one – was seldom far away.

'I'm pushed for time now,' he said, 'but I can make some later. Why don't you give me the fundamentals of the situation now, and then – will twelve midnight be too late?'

Pence's eyes were like beacons in his dark face.

'Not for me, sir!'

'Let's say the lounge of the Royal Bath Hotel,' Dawlish said.

'You're very good, sir.' Pence began to frown, and Dawlish motioned him back to his chair while he himself sat down. 'But the fundamentals – that's not easy. In fact I don't know them, sir. I suppose if the truth be told, I've just got a feeling.'

Dawlish said quietly: 'I've been known to have hunches myself.'

'That's what makes you the one man who might listen,' Pence declared. He put a thick, broad-fingered hand into the inside pocket of his coat. 'I suppose this is the nearest I have actually to a fundamental.' He drew out a plastic cover, wallet-size, opened this and extracted some newspaper clippings. One, when unfolded, was at least two columns in length. He handed this to Dawlish who saw photographs of a man, a woman and a child.

### FAMILY PERISH IN FIRE

Professor and Mrs. Ryall, and their two-year-old daughter Janet, died of suffocation when their cottage on the outskirts of Wilbury was destroyed by fire, says the coroner's verdict.

A new kind of insect repellent, which when heated at a certain low temperature can give off a noxious, lethal gas, was to blame.

The repellent is manufactured in Northern Ireland and imported into this country.

'All authorities should examine the repellent and its effects closely,' said Dr. Ingleson, the coroner. 'Otherwise many more tragedies such as this might occur.'

Evidence was given by . . .

Dawlish skimmed the rest of the report, including the fact that an empty tin had been found on the floor near the gas stove, supplies of natural gas having been available in the rural area of Wilbury only two years earlier. Arson experts from Birmingham, medical experts and local people, had all given testimony and a picture of a happy family emerged, making the tragedy seem even more poignant. There were details of the funeral, a list of individuals who had sent flowers, and there was one company named:

Flowers were also sent by the management of Astrid Limited as well as by the staff and fellow-workers at the Wilbury plant.

Dawlish looked up. 'Astrid?'

'The aeronautical experimental firm, sir.'

'Wasn't there a rumour that they had found a way to silence jets?'

'Yes, sir – premature release.'

'But true?'

'There is a certain amount of evidence to that effect, sir.'

'Was Professor Ryall involved?'

'More than that – he was the key researcher, sir. Regarded

by many as one of the most brilliant men in British aero-nautics.'

'Well, well,' Dawlish said, and glanced at the other clippings. These were from *The Times*, the *Daily Telegraph* and *The Aeronaut*, all tributes to Ryall's contribution to the development of aircraft in England. Dawlish was aware of time passing too quickly, but took no heed. 'You don't agree with accidental death?'

'I don't mind admitting I've done absolutely everything I can to find a flaw in the evidence,' stated Pence, his voice sounding as ruthless as it was harsh. 'I haven't been able to uncover a thing. Not a single thing. On the evidence, Dr. Ingleson returned the only possible verdict.'

Dawlish looked at him for a long time, before asking: 'What does your hunch say?'

'That about the same time as this tragedy four of a team of eight men working on the project resigned to take up jobs said to be in America. Hush-hush jobs. Ryall was streets ahead of any one of them but he wouldn't leave the country.'

'Wouldn't?'

'Flat refusal,' replied Pence.

'Evidence?'

'He was overheard in the Royal Wilbury Arms. A man had hired a private room, and passing outside the door a waiter overheard Ryall's refusal. He particularly noted the reason: "because he was English".'

'When was this?' demanded Dawlish.

'The very day of the fire, sir – four weeks ago.'

'And the other men?'

'Packed up and gone.'

'And the silent jet project?'

'In cold storage,' answered Pence, flatly. 'Without those four men in the team it has to be. Some formulae were left behind but the project's been put back at least two years. The management is pretty sick about it, they had an enormous commercial as well as military market eager to buy.'

'Has the management done anything?' asked Dawlish.

'Not really,' answered Pence. 'No, you couldn't say it had. This question of the brain drain is very serious in certain industries, and none more so than the aircraft and motor manufacturing industries. Astrid's just accept the fact that American companies have bought their best men out. They aren't convinced that Ryall wouldn't have gone, they think he was holding out for more money. They don't take me seriously when I so much as hint that Ryall's death might have been murder.'

Pence stopped.

Dawlish looked from the dead man's photograph to Pence, and pursed his lips. He was convinced that Pence believed absolutely in his hunch. He decided that the matter needed careful thought; more than he could give it at the moment. But there was no apparent need for urgency – not for a few hours, anyway.

'One more question,' he said. 'Can you support your hunch?'

'I can rationalize it, sir, if that's what you mean.'

'That's good enough,' declared Dawlish. 'Now come in and have a drink, I'm sure you'll be welcome.'

'If you don't mind, sir, I won't,' said Pence, to his surprise. 'It's very nice of you but – well, I think the fewer people who know I've been down here to see you, the better. A lot of the senior officers will know me from Yard days. Mr. Moss promised to keep it confidential.'

'Right!' Dawlish was brisk. 'Midnight, then, at the Royal Bath Hotel. We'll find a spot where we can talk quietly.'

'Thank you, Mr. Dawlish,' Pence said, his voice warmer than it had been before. 'I'm very grateful. Just one other thing before I go.'

'Yes?'

'The way some of our best brains are being bribed to go abroad is absolutely disastrous, sir. And nothing's being done about it. It's not only America. You'd never believe how much is going on.' Pence broke off, and then his rock-like face broke into a broad smile. 'But that's where I'm wrong, sir! You *would* believe.'

He held out his hand, and Dawlish gripped it, sensing that the gesture meant a great deal to the other man.

He had only ten minutes left with the Bournemouth Police, and was amused to find Felicity the centre of half a dozen men, all throwing questions at her; and as he drew nearer he realized that the questions were about him.

'What is it like living with him, Mrs. Dawlish?'

'Has he changed at all since he became a policeman?'

'Is there any aspect of his work which he seems to prefer to any other?'

'Yes,' boomed Dawlish. 'Two things. One: protecting my wife. Two: talking shop.'

There was a general laugh; the waitress offered him another drink. Moss was obviously keeping a very close eye on the clock, and the informal party broke up at seven-ten precisely.

Ten minutes later they entered a big red-brick house on the West Cliff, and across the shimmering blue sea saw the magnificent views of Bournemouth Bay and even of the Isle of Wight in the evening sun which shone from an almost cloudless sky.

Dawlish enjoyed the evening immensely, and Felicity obviously took to Osgood's wife – his second wife, who was twenty years or so younger than her husband. Two married sons and their wives and two teenage grandsons made up the party, and after a long time of talking about the past and swapping parachute jumps and escape stories Osgood himself suddenly changed the subject.

'Pat, let me ask you a question which I often ask myself. Now that you can look back on the war, do you think it served a purpose? Are we as a country, and is the world at large, better off? Or was the war really fought in vain?'

'Oh, no,' Dawlish said, in a shocked reflex action. 'Not in vain. It won another chance for what we've always believed in – a chance to make a better place. Now if you were to ask me whether we've made the best use of that chance, that's another matter.'

'Honestly, sir,' said one of Osgood's grandsons, 'isn't it a *worse* world? I mean, isn't there much more crime? I mean,' he went on earnestly, fighting back his embarrassment, 'would you have a job, or rather would you have the job you're in now, if crime hadn't shot sky-high? It's bad enough country by country but when you have to have an international police force to fight international criminals – well, isn't it really another kind of war?'

## CHAPTER FOUR

## ANOTHER KIND OF WAR

THROUGHOUT the evening, Dawlish had sensed the disillusion in this family, and had no doubt that it had started with Osgood himself and his shattered knee. Osgood had gone from the European zone to Burma and India; and as one of those who had taken part in a war against the Japanese, and fought in the fetid jungles, had suffered more than most. After his years of unbelievable endurance and courage fighting a war he had believed in, he had been brought to the conclusion that it had been without purpose.

He nodded as his grandson spoke, and said 'Hear, hear' as that last challenging question came. 'Well – isn't it really another kind of war?'

Everyone at the table, except Felicity, looked at Dawlish as if expecting him to disagree.

'Yes, of course,' he answered flatly.

'*You* think that?' the grandson gasped, and Osgood looked astonished.

'I've thought so for a long time,' Dawlish replied crisply. 'In some ways it's worse, because we don't always know the enemy, and worse still because it's a kind of civil war. Still, I'd rather fight this war than the other kind, and if we could get rid of the other kind – even the threat of it – we'd have much more chance to win the one that keeps me awake at night. But enough of this philosophizing! Next question – which of you youngsters has the cock-eyed idea that the police are against the people?'

'A lot of college students in America believe it,' the other grandson declared.

'After that bit of bother we had last year on campuses all round the world\* most of them have dropped the notion. That was a fascinating case!' Dawlish launched into a story of campus riots and disorders on all continents, and how this had led to the Crime Haters setting up their head-

\* *A Rabble of Rebels*

quarters in a small and little-known estate. He had them all enthralled until twenty to twelve, when he glanced at the clock and exclaimed:

'Look at that time! I've someone coming to see me at the stroke of midnight.'

The young men said good night and went off. As the Dawlishes got up to leave, the sound of a trumpet, played high and pure, came clearly into the room. It was unusual enough to make Felicity exclaim at its beauty.

'That's David,' Mrs. Osgood said. David was the grandson who had asked about the war. 'He plays in a band, and never loses a chance to practise.'

'You're honoured,' Osgood said. 'Most unusual for him to stay with us after a meal. Never heard the trumpet played better, not even in the Far East.'

Dawlish's car, an old Bentley, was in the drive, brought here from the Dean Park parking ground by a police driver. Most of the family stood on the drive to see Felicity and him off. As he turned into West Cliff Drive, with its imposing houses and tall trees and, near the pier, its big hotels and the myriad small ones, Felicity slid her arm through his.

'Such a diplomat, darling.'

'Did I do all right?'

'Ten years ago you would have asked that silly adolescent if he was English or not!'

'Not if Ossy was listening and looking on,' declared Dawlish. 'He really is taking the world situation hard.'

'His wife told me that he's in almost constant pain with his knee,' remarked Felicity. 'And he had some chest illness which left him with asthma, too. Did you notice the smell of herbal cigarettes?'

'I noticed something,' Dawlish admitted.

'It's a herb he smokes for relief from asthma,' Felicity explained, and then went on thoughtfully: 'I suppose it does make one wonder what fighting is all about.'

'Does it?' asked Dawlish, as he stopped at a T-junction at the foot of a hill, allowing a stream of cars to pass.

Felicity did not answer, and Dawlish turned right, past the pier festooned with lights, past two groups of pop singers and guitar players holding an impromptu concert at the approaches to the pier under the benevolent gaze of at least four policemen. Soon they were heading up the hill alongside

27

the white shape of the Royal Bath Hotel – and, wonder of wonders, there was a policeman standing by a vacant parking space.

'Thought you'd soon be along, sir,' the policeman said in greeting, 'so when a man pulled out I kept the place for you.'

'You're very good,' Dawlish said. 'Thank you.'

He and Felicity walked on to the hotel, then stood on the steps leading down into the lounge with its great picture windows overlooking the gardens and the moonlit sea. A clock struck twelve.

'Ah,' Dawlish said, heading for the windows. 'My man will be here in about thirty seconds.'

'Are you as sure of him as that?'

'A man who's gone to all the trouble he has isn't likely to be late,' Dawlish declared confidently. He glanced over his shoulder, as if seriously expecting to see Pence. 'Do you want to be in on the session, darling?'

'Do you want me to be?'

'It might inhibit the other chap.'

'I'll go over to that corner and look through some magazines,' Felicity volunteered. It was characteristic of her not to complain that she was tired, or to expect explanations.

'Thank you, darling,' Dawlish said.

He watched her for a few seconds – seconds which had a significance beyond all conception. For when he looked into the garden he saw two men – one walking towards the hotel windows, and one springing from behind a bush with his hand raised high; it was even possible to see that he had a weapon in it.

'Look out!' cried Dawlish in a stentorian voice. '*Look out!*'

The weapon fell.

The man who had been coming towards the hotel staggered.

The weapon was raised again.

Dawlish leapt towards the window and banged with his clenched fist; it gave a hollow, booming sound. The staggering man fell, his assailant paused to look round. Dawlish struck the window again.

A waiter came running. 'Zis way, zir.' He sprang past Dawlish to a door at the side of the window, pulling a key from his pocket. Dawlish went after him, waiting only for the door to swing open. He ran out, shouting:

'Stop that! Stop that!'

There was a man on the ground, and there was the one bending over him, arm and weapon raised. But he did not strike again. As Dawlish approached, he turned and ran towards the garden wall where it divided the hotel grounds from the cliff walk, and vaulted over it.

'Look after him!' Dawlish roared, pointing at the man on the ground. He glanced over his shoulder and saw the waiter, Felicity and two men streaming out of the doorway.

Dawlish raced over springy grass, round bushes and flower-beds, across a gravel path. He saw the assailant running down the cliff walk. The moonlight showed all obstacles and also showed the wall. Dawlish cleared it like a hurdler, and went racing after the man.

Then he saw another man step from a gateway.

On a darker night he could not have been so sure of what was happening, but now the moon shone on a face half-covered by a scarf; pale hands: and a gun in one of them.

Dawlish flung himself forward, hands outstretched. He heard the crack of a shot but felt nothing, rolled over, heard another crack and felt something tug at his coat sleeve. Next moment a car engine started up, a man shouted, foot-steps clattered, Felicity called out:

'*Pat!* Darling! Pat!'

Footsteps drew nearer. He raised his head and saw a small car, without lights, racing down the hill and knew there was no hope of catching it. The waiter was only a few yards away, Felicity not far behind, a big man a little way behind her. Dawlish got up on one knee as the waiter cried:

'You are hurt, bad?'

'I'm not hurt at all,' Dawlish replied in a carrying voice. 'Wouldn't allow such a thing, would I, darling?' By the time Felicity drew up he was on his feet, looking now towards the grounds of the hotel. Lights streamed out from doors and windows, and a torch shone on a group of three men, one lying and two kneeling on the ground. He put his arm about Felicity's waist, and hurried her along to the wall. Then, shifting his hold, he lifted her and placed her on her feet on the other side. Vaulting over himself, he asked her to wait for him, and sprinted twenty yards ahead to the little group of three.

The man on the grass was Pence.

His eyes were closed and his mouth slack. Blood flowed from a wound on his forehead and another at the side of his neck.

'Is a doctor on the way?' Dawlish asked.

'The hotel doctor will be here in a minute,' one of the others said.

Dawlish padded a handkerchief and pressed it against the neck wound, while with his free hand he felt for Pence's pulse. It was quite strong. The wound on the forehead did not look serious, but the neck wound could prove fatal.

Soon, the doctor came hurrying, closely followed by a policeman.

In five minutes Pence was on a stretcher being carried to an ambulance which had pulled up on the cliff drive, and the doctor was saying to Dawlish:

'It missed the carotid by a fraction, but for that he wouldn't have a chance. Should do all right now, with care.' He looked more intently at Dawlish. 'You are the chap who won our open tennis, aren't you?'

'Yes.'

'Saw you on television tonight,' the doctor told him. 'Do you attract trouble wherever you go, Mr. Dawlish, or does it follow you around?'

'Now that's a good question,' Dawlish said. 'When would you expect the victim to be able to speak?'

'Now that's an even better question,' the doctor retorted, smiling. 'I've given him a shot which will keep him under for at least six hours, and I imagine the hospital medicos will want at least as long again. I'm sorry I can't be more precise.'

'You're very good,' said Dawlish gratefully. 'Will you go with him in the ambulance?'

'I can.'

'Will you, please?'

'Very well,' the other agreed, without asking questions.

'I should warn you that I expect trouble to follow him,' Dawlish said.

The doctor nodded, outwardly unconcerned.

Already a police car was coming up the cliff drive, giving a wide berth to a spot protected by two of the men from the hotel; the spot where Dawlish had been shot at. Another police car came in sight, and a third from the other direction, following the ambulance. Dawlish watched these drive off, and then turned to Felicity.

'Sweet, I'm going to be late, I'm afraid.'

'I can see you are. Let me take the car, and—'

'No,' Dawlish interrupted. 'This is not the night for you to go anywhere alone. I wonder if the hotel has a room.'

'We most certainly have, Mr. Dawlish,' said a man wearing a dressing-gown over pyjamas. 'I am the assistant manager, Soames, and I can have a double room prepared in less than ten minutes. If you and Mrs. Dawlish care to come with me . . .'

It was a large room with bathroom and balcony. Felicity, shocked and tired, was more than ready for bed. Dawlish left her and went downstairs to find Superintendent Moss in the grounds, a dozen plain-clothes men already busy, flashlights and some floodlights already trained on the scene of the attack.

Police were at the hospital and a man would sit with Pence until he came round, while another would be outside the door. The hotel was guarded back and front, and the Dawlishes' room, also. All of these things had been done with a minimum of fuss.

Now Moss was saying:

'There isn't much doubt he would have been killed if you hadn't looked outside when you did, sir.'

'No,' Dawlish agreed.

'And you got away with it lightly.' Moss touched a tear in the right sleeve of Dawlish's jacket, close to the shoulder. 'You know what that is, don't you?'

'Bullet tear,' Dawlish said equably.

'Do you think they'll try again?' asked Moss.

'The truth is that I don't know, and I'd be glad if you'd take all precautions,' Dawlish said. 'If we can get a clue to either of the assailants we'll be on our way. As for what it is . . .' He smiled down at the local superintendent. 'Pence said he thought he was on to a new form of international industrial espionage. He took a lot of trouble to hide the fact that he was coming to see me, but these jokers must have followed, guessed what he'd done at your headquarters, and tried to make sure he couldn't tell me any more. Whether they

31

attacked me because they wanted me dead, or whether it was simply to stop me from catching them, I don't know – yet,' he added grimly. 'Can you let me have a room at your headquarters? I ought to get in touch with my people in London and start some inquiries.'

'You won't mind if I have you driven over?' Moss said. 'I would like to stay here.'

'You're very kind,' Dawlish said. He seemed to be saying that to everyone. In a way it was a brake on the tearing desire within him to start work on Pence's hunch, which was now very much more than a hunch – it was the real thing.

Dawlish felt as sure as Pence that the death of the Ryalls had been no accident. And if these unknown chaps could be so cold-blooded as to massacre a family, and then make a murderous attack on Pence, they were evil indeed. Dawlish realized that in all probability he was on the threshold of a major battle in that 'other kind of war'.

CHAPTER FIVE

## CRIME HATERS – LONDON

AT one time the headquarters of the Crime Haters in London had been managed by a middle-aged man, Childs, who had retired two years ago, and never been satisfactorily replaced. This was one of Dawlish's main problems. He had as second-in-command a younger man named Gordon Scott, but Scott was a man with a roving disposition, and a yearning to be out of doors.

Childs, on the other hand, had been satisfied to sit at the hub and watch whatever was happening outside from within, while keeping in close contact not only with Dawlish's men but with the Crime Haters throughout the world.

But Childs was gone, and Scott was often stand-in at these headquarters.

He was a man in his middle thirties, had been transferred from the straightforward C.I.D. work of the Yard to Dawlish at his own and Dawlish's request, and even when the sedentary work chafed he took great pride in his job.

That night he was in the offices.

These were on top of the old building at New Scotland Yard, close to Whitehall, the Thames and Big Ben, and the whole floor had been given over to the Crime Haters – or to give it a more formal title: *The Department of International Criminal Investigation Liaison.* One section, used by Dawlish, had two huge panels, one a relief map of the world, in sections, on which was marked every agent of the Crime Haters. Every city and town which had an agent or liaison officer was shown as a dot which would light up red if an incoming call, and light up green if an outgoing call were made. Telecommunication was possible with each within ten seconds.

One area, marked differently from the rest, was now the headquarters of the Police Conference, where a small regular secretariat worked. It was close to the capital of Golana, and controlled by a remarkable South American woman named Camilla Felista. The main problem was finding funds to keep this going, but so far that had been accomplished.

The second panel was used to show special calls and cases. It had shown every town and city in which there had been campus troubles during the days of that investigation.

At the moment this panel was empty.

The moment was one o'clock in the morning.

Scott was on night duty by his own choice. Engaged to marry a girl who was out of England for a few weeks, he took a chance which would enable him to work more normal hours when she was home. Not that 'normal hours' meant very much to the Crime Haters. In times of crisis a twenty-hour working day for seven days a week was 'normal'.

A night staff was busy in the rest of the department, which was always kept at a hundred per cent running efficiency. Half the world's night was the other half's day. Scott was checking a report from West Germany about industrial diamonds which were being stolen on a large scale, when a telephone bell rang. A glance showed him that this was a call from somewhere in England. It crossed his mind that it might be Dawlish; he had expected Dawlish to ask him why

33

he had wished old Pence on to him on the second honeymoon he was having with his wife.

Second? Or hundred and second.

'Gordon Scott, International Office.'

'You mean you're not out looking for someone to send down to me tomorrow?' Dawlish asked.

'Oh, hallo, sir! No indeed, sir! Last thing I'd do.' Scott, a handsome man in a rather rugged way, became slightly confused.

'How well do you know Pence?' asked Dawlish.

'One of my first sergeants in the force, sir, and I was a detective sergeant under him for several years. Absolutely first-class as a man and a cop-detective, sir.' When Dawlish didn't comment he went on: 'He lost his wife about three years ago. Hit him very hard. He said he couldn't stay in London, where they'd been all their married life, that's why he went to the Midlands and Astrid's. You don't doubt him, do you?'

'He told me a little, I arranged to see him later, and he was attacked. He's at Boscombe Hospital now.'

'Good God!' exclaimed Scott. 'How is he?'

'He'll recover, but slowly.'

'One good thing,' said Scott, still shaken.

'How often did he have hunches?'

'Old *Pence*, sir? *Hunches?*'

'Yes.'

'Absolute stickler for facts and evidence. He kept his own card index and cross-index systems to relate crimes to criminals. The ultimate professional, in fact. I remember once when he – ah – he, well, never mind, sir.' Scott had recalled an occasion when Chief Inspector Pence had told him what he thought of amateurs and hunches, specifying a certain Mr. Dawlish.

'Thanks,' Dawlish said. 'How much did he tell you?'

'Nothing, sir.' Scott eased his collar away from his neck, feeling more than a little uncomfortable. It was not often that Dawlish or anyone else caught him on the wrong foot, but he felt right off balance this time. 'I checked with Bournemouth and learned you were still in the tournament and I dithered – he really came the old soldier in a way, pulling his authority. He simply said he had something he could only discuss with you. Did he tell you?' Scott cleared his throat.

'A little,' Dawlish said, and his manner relaxed. 'All right, Gordon – here's a job I'd like you to do at once. Contact all our people in countries where they have a strong aeronautical and aircraft industry. That means the United States, France, Russia, Japan – all the big ones. Ask them if they've suffered much from the brain drain recently.'

'You mean we aren't the only ones who have?'

'You know better than that. Don't try for any specific details yet, just general information. I want to know whether any particular country and also whether any particular firm in any country has suffered worse than most.'

'What about England?' asked Gordon Scott bluntly, repenting the words as soon as they were spoken. This was no night on which to show how clever he was.

'Pence almost certainly has an index file on the situation in England,' Dawlish replied drily. 'All clear and understood?'

'Yes, sir.'

'I'm staying at the Royal Bath Hotel in Bournemouth,' Dawlish went on. 'Call me if you think there's the slightest need.'

'I will, sir,' promised Scott, and then an idea seemed to seize him, and he was on the point of telling Dawlish when he hesitated. Dawlish did not overlook the obvious and he, Scott, had put his foot in it too often already. Yet . . .

'What's worrying you?' Dawlish asked.

'Well, I don't know that worry is the word—'

'Gordon,' interrupted Dawlish, 'I'm tired out and I'm probably suffering from delayed shock and no doubt I am in a foul humour, but you are particularly exasperating tonight. Is there anything on your mind or isn't there?'

Stung, Gordon said: 'Yes, sir.'

'Then what is it?'

'If ex-Chief Inspector Pence has been attacked in person,' went on Gordon stiffly, and he glowered at a picture of Dawlish with a group of delegates to the International Police Conference from many parts of the world, 'would his home or his office be attacked, too? Other people may know about his cross-indexes.'

'My God!' breathed Dawlish. 'I didn't think of that. Call Birmingham and Wilbury. Have the factory and his home closely guarded. Hurry.'

'Yes, sir!' said Scott, savouring a moment of quiet triumph.

Pence lived in a large room in a small hotel in Wilbury. It had been ransacked and there was no way of telling what had been taken away.

His office at the Astrid factory had not been touched; and no attempt was made to force entry during the night.

Dawlish wondered what was getting under his skin.

It was useless to tell himself that he was overtired, and that two days of extreme physical exertion were enough in themselves to explain it. There was something else. He might have blamed it on to the attack on Pence, even more on the fact that if he'd gone to the window half a minute earlier he might have stopped the assault altogether. But that wasn't it: he had felt it most of the evening, certainly before the Osgood grandson had fired his loaded question. True, he had taken the wind out of the young man's sails, but the question itself went a long way to explaining his mood.

That, and Ossy's agreement with it.

It wasn't good that a man who had given so much for his country should become so disillusioned that he doubted whether the effort had been worth while. That Colonel Reginald Osgood, D.S.O., M.C. (and bar), *Croix de Guerre*, Belgian, Dutch and Danish honours, hero of some of the most breathtaking episodes during the war, should think that all his efforts and his sacrifices had been in vain.

Did Ossy really think so?

Had his sons and his grandsons worked on him until he felt shame instead of pride in what he had done behind the Nazi and the Japanese lines, organizing escapes, sabotaging railway lines and roads and ammunition dumps, playing a leading part in organizing the resistance which, in the long run, had done so much to wear down the enemy's will to win?

'And the truth is,' he told himself as he stepped out of the lift at the Royal Bath, 'that I didn't meet it head on. Not really. I told them a morality story instead.'

'What's that, sir?' asked a young plain-clothes man just outside his bedroom.

Dawlish smiled.

'Talking to myself, the first sign of senility, don't they say?'

'Do they, sir? Congratulations on your game this afternoon.'

Dawlish's smile broadened.

'I must try and do this every year. Good night.'

'Good night, sir.'

Dawlish opened and closed the bedroom door quietly, and shot the bolt with hardly a sound. A light from the cliff walk spread soft radiance about the room, touching Felicity's pale face, which looked in sleep so young and vulnerable.

Careful not to wake her, he was in bed within five minutes.

It was already a quarter to three.

If only the evening at Ossy's hadn't been spoiled.

He almost wished he hadn't come.

Almost.


He felt stirring beside him.

He opened his left eye a fraction so that he could see through his lashes.

He was aware of daylight, dimmed as by blinds; of the stirring beside him again.

Of Felicity.

He opened his other eye. How dear she was to him.

'Darling, did I wake you?'

He said truthfully: 'I wasn't really asleep.'

'You're worried, aren't you?'

'A little.'

'It's the Osgoods, isn't it?'

'Well, yes.'

Felicity said quietly: 'What is it about them that disturbs you?'

'That's just it, I don't *know*.' He added a little fretfully: 'I thought perhaps *you* might.'

Not wanting him to see how touched she was, she said carefully: 'I *think* it is because they have no faith.'

He moved restlessly.

'Oh, it's not religion, it—'

'I didn't mean religious faith,' Felicity interrupted. 'Pat, you're the most old-fashioned patriot alive, even though you do believe in a world police force. It still shakes you to think there are Englishmen who've changed their ideas.' When he

37

didn't comment, she went on: 'Do you have any idea what I'm talking about?'

He grinned, 'Yes, indeed. You are calling me an anachronism waving a Union Jack.'

'No,' denied Felicity, 'it isn't a matter of country any longer. It's a question a lot of people ask themselves: is what the West calls freedom, is what we call democracy, really all it's been said to be? Has it been worth the tens of millions of lives lost to preserve it?'

Dawlish lay looking at her, then very gently he kissed her eyes, so that she could not open them. It was as if he did not want her to see the bleakness in his. After a while he drew back, and stretched out for the telephone on the bedside table. He asked for Boscombe Hospital, waited, then asked for the police officer on duty in the main hall, and when this man answered in a gruff voice, he asked:

'This is Dawlish. How is the man I sent in last night?'

'Had a very good night, sir,' the policeman reported, 'in fact I was talking to the ward sister only ten minutes ago. Apparently he's out of danger.'

So it would not be long before ex-Chief Inspector Pence was able to tell him more about his hunch.


CHAPTER SIX

LONDON


DAWLISH drank morning tea with Felicity, had a leisurely bath, then talked to Moss while Felicity was bathing and getting ready. Moss had many things to report, all of them negative. The police had found two spent cartridges but couldn't identify the gun they had been fired from. They had found footprints of the men who had been involved in last night's attacks, also tyreprints of the car presumably used by them, but although photographs of these were being sent to police stations and garages, nothing had been traced. The weapon used to attack Hugo Pence had not been found.

'And the car?' asked Dawlish.

'We think it was a sports car with the hood down,' answered Moss. He sounded tired, and as if he had to keep a tight rein on his temper. 'We've sent a description to the Yard, of course, it will have been widely distributed by now. Will you stay at the cottage or stay at the Royal Bath?'

'Go home, I think,' Dawlish answered.

'I'll see you're protected up to the Surrey border,' promised Moss.

'Thanks,' Dawlish said. 'Just as well to be sure, and who knows what we might pick up if I'm followed. I'll drive to the New Forest cottage first.'

'You needn't worry about anything going wrong there,' Moss assured him. 'I've had it watched all night. No one made any attempt to break in.' He paused, and then exploded: 'I've done everything I know how, and haven't helped with a damned thing!'

'Just saved the odd life or two,' Dawlish remarked. 'Mine for instance. Thanks, Superintendent. I've never been so glad to deal with a man on top of his job.'

He rang off before Moss had time to comment, and gave a lopsided grin as he crossed to Felicity, who was sitting at the dressing-table mirror and making do with the meagre cosmetics from her handbag. As he bent down to kiss the back of her neck, she asked suspiciously:

'What have you been up to?'

'Don't be so suspicious,' Dawlish answered with a grin. 'We could have breakfast on the balcony, but wherever we sit we'll have a full view of the police searching for clues.'

Felicity looked at his reflection in the mirror, and then her face brightened.

'Why don't we drive back, and I'll cook something at the cottage?'

'There's no doubt I married the right woman!' Dawlish approved. 'That's exactly what we'll do.'

The drive through the New Forest, its trees heavy with leaf and a few already turning colour, was balm. The sight of the little cottage with its weathered walls and lichen-covered roof, was fresh pleasure.

They ate a gay and leisurely meal, then Dawlish tidied things about the house while Felicity washed up and cleared the kitchen. By twelve o'clock, two suitcases piled into the back of the Bentley, they started off for London. They talked very little, and if Felicity noticed how often Dawlish glanced into the driving mirror to see if they were being followed, she didn't comment.

They were on the Staines by-pass when she asked:

'Do you feel better now, Pat?'

'I'm less edgy,' he admitted. 'I suppose I shall always wish it hadn't happened.' He snatched a glance from the road and grinned at her, gay and carefree. 'You didn't realize I was a hero-worshipper, did you?'

'And you hero-worshipped Ossy?'

'A near thing,' he told her. 'Now – *zoom*.' He put his foot down on the accelerator and they roared past cars which were mere striplings in comparison to the ancient Bentley. 'There's life in the old dog yet,' he boasted.

Then he saw the car in front of them inexplicably change course.

It was an old Austin, square-backed, black, and suddenly it swerved across the road. Dawlish trod on the brakes; they screamed. The Austin was veering now this way, now that, seldom leaving passing room on either side. Cars coming up from behind squealed to slow down, horns blared.

The Austin shot across the road, and stopped, blocking both lanes.

It had no driver.

Dawlish was only a few yards away from the Austin.

He had been driving fast, and the slowing down seemed to last for ever. He saw cars swinging right and left behind him, but apart from the Austin the road in front was clear.

He clutched the handbrake, said: 'Hold tight,' as if Felicity were not already holding on to seat and car door like grim death. The Bentley shuddered and seemed to choke. Dawlish eased off the brakes and turned the wheel; there was just room to pass on the left-hand side. He felt the handle scrape the wing of the car as he got by. He went on a few yards, feeling cold and clammy, not quite sure how he had managed to avoid a crash.

Out of the corner of his eye he saw a car streaking towards the spot, ignoring the grouped cars and the obvious emergency. The driver must have been blinded by one car or another, for he squeezed through a narrow gap – and smashed into the Austin.

The Austin blew up, and the small car with it.

Dawlish saw the horrifying scene in his driving mirror.

The explosion began in the Austin, at the steering wheel. One great sheet of flame, a fierce explosion, a billow of dark grey smoke.

Pieces of metal struck the top of the Bentley and stabbed into the bonnet. The car was lifted off the ground, rocked wildly, swung round facing the scene of the explosion, dropped on to all four wheels and steadied. Only a car of its size and weight could have suffered so little. Dawlish had an arm round Felicity's shoulders, crushing her to him as if they were one body. Both of them were too shocked to speak.

For the blast and the flames had engulfed other cars.

Not just the two directly involved were ablaze but at least three others. And flung over the top of one was the broken body of a man.

The heat from the fire came in waves towards the Bentley. Dawlish began to move, tried the handle of the driving door, but found the door jammed, tried again and could not shift it. Drivers from cars on the other carriageway were now leaving their cars and some were trying to help, but the flames beat them back. A police siren was screaming, and another sounded in the distance. One police car pulled across to the Bentley.

'Get to the side, please, sir, and wait.'

'Assistant Commissioner Dawlish,' Dawlish said, and saw the man's start of recognition. 'I must get on – give my door a tug for me, will you?' As the man gripped the handle and pulled, Dawlish went on: 'Will you tell *Information* to advise the Bournemouth Police to treble their watch on Mr. Pence? They'll know what you mean.'

The driver of the police car already had the radio-telephone in his hand.

He sent the message, the other man eased the door open and closed it again. 'It wants pulling towards you before being pushed out, sir,' He spoke mechanically, the driver talked in the same way, horror, as well as the glow of the fire, reflected in their eyes.

Half a mile along the road everything was normal; traffic passed, some fast, some slow. Two aircraft above their heads prepared to land at Heathrow.

'Pat,' Felicity said, 'it was meant for you, wasn't it?'

'Us,' Dawlish said, gruffly.

'And there *wasn't* a driver?'

'Remote control. Could be some distance away, could have been from one of the cars behind me. Like me to pull in and get a brandy?'

'I'd rather go straight home.'

'So would I.' Felicity was silent for a few minutes before she went on: 'Did it start with Pence coming to see you?'

'My part in it did,' Dawlish answered.

'Pat, darling, you don't have to lie. Did you have any idea before?'

He put a hand on her knee: a big, well-shaped hand.

'No lies, sweetheart. No evasions. I had no ulterior motive in going to Bournemouth. Pence used to be Gordon Scott's boss at the Yard, and . . .' Dawlish explained as much as he knew, and then went on: 'Pence was followed and watched, and when he came to the Bournemouth police station while I was there his watchers put two and two together. They can't know how long we spent talking.'

He caught his breath.

'What's the matter?' Felicity demanded.

'They could know if someone told them,' Dawlish said.

'But who would?'

'A policeman could have.'

'You surely don't think – ' Felicity broke off.

She had known, as had he, times when corruption had eaten into some police forces. One man here, another there, taking a bribe for a piece of information. To say that it could not happen was ludicrous. Once, the whole of the Metropolitan Police Force of London had been suspect.* All that was needed was one frail human being, and the rot began.

Dawlish said gruffly: 'There could have been a leakage. There were some reporters there, too, and reporters are very friendly with the Bournemouth Police.'

'Was that girl Sue What's-her-name there?'

*A Nest of Traitors*

Dawlish was surprised into a grin.

'I didn't notice Sue Day and I'll wager she would have made sure I did if she'd been there. The point is' – he negotiated the turn-off from the Great West Road to the M4 before going on – 'that these people appear to have wiped out a whole family in the Midlands, tried to kill Pence because he was the only man who really believed the deaths were murder and not accidental, and now have risked killing dozens of motorists who could not possibly be involved, so as to make sure I can't probe into whatever Pence told me.' He was silent for a few minutes, and then went on: 'Can you stand being watched and followed wherever you go for a while?'

'It won't be exactly a new experience,' Felicity said, drily.

'Bless you. And I'm going to take you up to the flat and then leave you for a while.'

The Dawlishes had a penthouse apartment atop a new office building near Millbank, overlooking the Thames. Its views over London were magnificent, and yet it was so high up it seemed remote from the bustling world below.

Policemen were already on duty at the main entrance, which was reached by a crescent-shaped carriageway from the Embankment. In the foyer and in the hall outside the apartment itself were more policemen. One of the two men upstairs took the suitcases. Dawlish was in the apartment for no more than ten minutes, and then he left for his office, only ten minutes' walk away.

'Going to drive or be driven?' asked a plain-clothes man.

'Walk,' Dawlish answered.

'Are you sure that's wise, sir, after what happened on the Staines by pass?'

Dawlish smiled faintly. 'I'm sure it's not wise to try to keep out of sight of assailants every moment. I'll be all right. Are you my bodyguard?'

'One of them. I'm Harris, sir.'

'Keep fifty yards behind,' Dawlish said. 'I won't run away and they say I'm easy to pick out in a crowd.'

The man smiled; he had very good teeth, and Dawlish rather took to him.

London looked good in the early-afternoon sunshine.

Trippers and sightseers thronged Parliament Square and

Westminster Bridge. The river trips were having an un-expected burst of late summer business. There was comparatively little car traffic but masses of buses and coaches. Policemen were everywhere, several surrounded by groups of inquiring tourists. Few glanced up as Dawlish strode past the Abbey, crossed to the yard at the Houses of Parliament, went to the approach to Westminster Bridge and crossed at the lights to the Embankment. Here the crowds had thinned to practically a trickle.

He turned into the Embankment gates of New Scotland Yard, and as he did so, he noticed two things.

Parked only a few yards from the gates was a dark green M.G. with its hood down. Standing by this was a slim, young-looking man with a newspaper in his hand. Dawlish did not check his stride, did nothing to show that he had taken any notice, took three more steps towards the open gates and then broke into a run. Standing behind the gates and hidden by the wall was another small, youngish-looking man, whose hand swiftly left his pocket. Three shots rang out loud and clear. Dawlish simply leapt towards his assailant, then dived, hands outstretched for his ankles.

He clutched them and jerked; and the man toppled backwards, the gun skidding along the ground. A man shouted, a car engine roared. Policemen came hurrying from the Yard.

'Watch him!' Dawlish scrambled to his feet and ran back through the gateway, and as he reached the Embankment the M.G. roared off along it. Dawlish had a fleeting glimpse of Harris half-in and half-out of a taxi, before it set out in hot pursuit.

## CHAPTER SEVEN

PRISONER

DAWLISH stopped running.

He was breathless with the sudden exertion, and brushing himself down, saw that there was a rent in one trouser leg and a red stain. The graze was painful, but not serious, he decided. Two men held the man who had fired at him. With a swift movement one of them snapped handcuffs to the prisoner's wrists.

Dawlish looked at the prisoner closely.

He had narrow features, was good-looking in a ferrety way, had dark hair brushed straight back from a prominent forehead. The eyes were dark, almost black.

He felt sure this was the man who had fired at him on the cliff walk.

It would make things so much easier if he could have him sent to the apartment, or to the flat of a friend, anywhere he could interrogate the man in his own way. In the days before he had become a policeman he had gained information—

Dreams!

And with the police behind him he had far more advantages than he had ever had in the days of his lone wolfing.

'Take him up to my office,' he said. 'Keep him closely guarded. Don't let him put anything in his mouth.'

The man to whom the prisoner was handcuffed said: 'Very good, sir.'

Dawlish turned to the prisoner: 'What's your name?'

The man did not answer. There was no telling whether his blank look meant that he did not understand the question, or that he was pretending not to. Dawlish watched him taken off, then went to the half a dozen men already checking the spot where the man had been lying in wait. They found two bullets but not the third. Dawlish took out the gun which he had slipped into his pocket.

'Point 22,' one of the others said.

Like last night's, reflected Dawlish. 'Can you spare a man to take it to the Yard and have ballistics check this bullet?' He took out one which Moss had given him, wrapped in a small plastic bag. 'I'd like to know as soon as possible whether the bullet in the bag was fired from this gun.'

'I'll have them call you,' the man promised, and turned and hurried off.

There was nothing more for Dawlish to do: every report would be made quickly, there was no need to prompt such men as these. He walked up the long stone staircase towards government offices now housed where the Metropolitan Police had once been, and up in a big, open trelliswork lift to the top floor. He stepped into a small, bare hall and crossed to his own room, marked *Deputy A.C.*, opened the door – and saw Gordon Scott [sitting at his, Dawlish's desk.

' 'Morning,' Dawlish said. 'Don't you ever sleep?'

'I was told what had happened on the Staines by-pass,' Scott replied, 'and I came straight in. Now I've heard what happened outside here. They really mean to get you, sir, don't they?'

'They certainly mean to try,' Dawlish said. 'What's the latest on Pence?'

'Good,' reported Scott, pushing the chair back and getting up. 'I've just been talking to Mr. Moss. Pence was lucky – the neck wound would have killed him if it had gone an inch deeper or half an inch to the left. As it is, he should be able to travel tomorrow.'

'We want him up today,' Dawlish decided. 'And we want the strongest guard we can think up for him.' He rounded the big, flat-topped desk and dropped into his chair. 'We've one prisoner, but I doubt if he's English and he certainly isn't going to speak English if he can help it.'

'I know, sir. He's in E room. Looks blank when anybody speaks to him.'

Dawlish shrugged. 'Just our luck. We take a prisoner and he's no good at all. Is Chumley in?' Chumley was the language genius at the Crime Haters H.Q.

'Yes, sir.'

'Have him go and see what he can do,' ordered Dawlish.

He had hardly finished when a light glowed on a panel on one side of his desk: this was direct communication from

46

New Scotland Yard, so he pressed a button and said: 'Dawlish.'

'Mr. Dawlish,' a man said formally, 'we've just had a report from City about the M.G.'

'Ah. What is it?'

'The driver got away, sir. The M.G. was found abandoned near the Barbican.'

'Well, that's something.'

'Where would you like us to take it, sir?'

'Scotland Yard first, and I'll talk to the Stolen Car Squad.'

The Stolen Car Squad had been in existence for a long time, and had become something much larger than its name implied. It operated a garage for maintenance of Yard cars as well as the examination of stolen vehicles, and could go over a car for prints, powder, dust, pieces of fabric, everything likely to be of use in a crime investigation, in a matter of minutes. 'Do you know what happened to my chap Harris?'

'He's on his way back, sir.'

'Thanks,' Dawlish said, and rang off. 'Gordon, Harris was detailed to watch me, but he raced off after one of the men involved, which would have left me stranded had I needed him. Make sure he doesn't do it again, will you?'

'Yes, sir.'

'What's he like, generally?'

'Mustard keen,' answered Scott.

'That could lead him into trouble. Are there any reports in from overseas?'

'I haven't checked yet, sir,' Scott replied. 'I've hardly been here five minutes.'

'Let's see,' Dawlish said. 'What's the code number?'

'C2, sir.'

When reports came in from the teleprinter section, just on the other side of this room, messages were fed automatically into several filing boxes; the computer system did the sorting, and while no action was taken on computer advice alone, it was invaluable for a quick survey.

About a dozen forms were in a box marked C2. Dawlish saw a note at the front: sixty-one inquiries had been sent out. He read the first reply, which was from Western Germany.

We have great difficulties retaining our research staff for both civil and military aircraft. Our loss – what you call the brain drain – is very serious. In one year at least twenty-two per cent of our best research workers have gone to America, Britain, Japan and France. Very great inducements are offered.

Kurt von Strohm

Von Strohm was one of the best men in the Crime Haters, a man who seemed to work round the clock.

Dawlish picked up the second, which was from Los Angeles, California.

The British certainly have the word for it – brain drain! Stockley Aircraft Corporation has lost nearly thirty per cent of its top research men in the past year. They go to other companies in the U.S.A., to Western Germany, Japan, and South America, and are paid the earth.

Lance Severid

The third reply said:

Considerable concern in my country at loss of research workers in aeroplane and automobile industries. Will gladly co-operate in any endeavour to prevent this. Stop. One very brilliant research worker who refused to go to the United States died in accident which might prove foul play. Endeavour please to inform me fullest and quickest way.

Hirito Sito

Dawlish dropped this one in front of Gordon Scott, who had read the others, and Scott whistled on a low key.

'I thought Japan and America were the villains,' he remarked. 'I knew a few of our chaps went to Europe, but – my God, sir, what have we stumbled on?'

'That's what we're finding out.'

The next cable was from Australia, where a large aircraft-manufacturing plant had recently been opened. It was from a government department: of Civil and Military Aviation.

We have recently been worried by the loss of certain of

our best research workers. One belief here is that this is a form of sabotage – a way of making sure we cannot compete with the major manufacturing companies in Europe, Japan and the United States. Some suspicion that China is developing a major aircraft industry and is bribing our staff but little credence given to this.

William Defoe, Minister

Dawlish also handed this to Scott, then pushed his chair back. A buzzing sound came from the feeding slot on the left and two more forms dropped with uncanny precision into C2. One was from Italy, one from Chicago, the giant Locking Aircraft Corporation.

Both expressed exactly the same fears.

Dawlish pulled a pad towards him and picked up a pencil, then made notes, often stating the obvious. Nations and corporations were – or declared themselves to be – deeply concerned about the brain drain, but it was by no means a one-way process. He made a list of headings of the different countries affected and a tick for each time a country was mentioned as the cause of some loss of research workers.

America was mentioned twenty-one times; Japan eighteen; Great Britain, surprisingly to him, was third, with sixteen. Down at the bottom of the list, with one apiece, was the Argentine and India.

'Come and have a look at this,' he said to Gordon Scott, and as Scott moved round to the desk, the telephone from New Scotland Yard buzzed. He picked it up.

'Dawlish,' he announced.

'Dawlish.' The repetition of his name was sufficient to tell him that this was the one man at Scotland Yard to whom he would always defer: Sir Arthur Winthrop, the commissioner. 'Are you all right?'

'No bones broken, anyhow,' Dawlish said, with forced lightness.

'Is it true that assassins were waiting for you as you went into your building?'

'Yes,' Dawlish answered.

'Do you know what it's about?' asked Winthrop.

'Yes and no,' replied Dawlish. He was aware of Gordon Scott watching intently: Gordon no doubt guessed who was on the line. 'I am quite sure there is a very powerful and ruthless organization which wanted to prevent me from reporting what little I have learned. They may stop now because they can't have any doubt what Pence told me is already on file.'

'Is it?'

'Enough to keep the inquiry going if I were to be disposed of,' Dawlish told him drily. 'Some things I know, some I've pieced together. Someone is trying to get the best aeronautical research men away from their plants and laboratories. It is on a major scale. I'm getting reports from all over the world that say the same thing. The man Pence, who may know more than he's yet told me, should be in London this afternoon and I'll have more reports in from overseas. But before then I'd like to release a statement.'

'Of what?'

'Saying just what I've told you,' Dawlish said simply. 'I can't think of any other way of telling the other side that they're not simply dealing with Great Britain but have the rest of the world on their heels. At least that—'

'Should take some of the pressure off you, and I am all for it,' interrupted the commissioner. 'I'd check with anyone affected and then put the story out, if I were you.'

'I'll do that,' Dawlish promised.

But as he rang off, and while he telephoned the Assistant Commissioner for Crime at New Scotland Yard, the restriction chafed. He had to go by the book, had to get the nominal approval of the man who was technically his superior, but sometimes there simply was not time.

This afternoon no one could have cut red tape more quickly, and he had the statement ready for the evening newspapers, television newscasts and radio broadcasts.

Not until this was done did he feel that he could breathe freely. When it was over, he went along to see the prisoner.

The man was still handcuffed. Perhaps it was the fluorescent lighting which made his eyes glint, as silver, and his face look so hawklike. Chumley, who was said to be fluent in twelve languages and to be acquainted with a dozen more, was sitting facing him. Knowing Chumley, Dawlish realized that he was both frustrated and exasperated. He got up as Dawlish entered, a tubby man with a plump face who looked shorter than he was because of his girth.

'Not a thing,' He answered Dawlish's unspoken inquiry. 'I've tried him on half a dozen languages but he hasn't said a word or given a sign of any kind.'

'Could he be deaf?' asked Dawlish.

'I suppose he could be,' replied Chumley, 'though he responds to unexpected noises. I'll keep at him, though.'

'Do that,' Dawlish said. 'The slightest clue as to where he comes from would help.'

'Pity you can't have a go at him yourself,' Chumley said. 'He might not stay so dumb if he was going to get hurt a bit.'

'Don't hurt him,' ordered Dawlish, and genial, kindly looking Chumley sighed. He turned into his office as Gordon Scott said into the telephone:

'Are you sure?... The great man's in no mood for guessing ... all right, all right, can't you take a joke? I'll tell him.' He replaced the receiver and looked up, beaming broadly. 'The bullets fired at you last night and the bullets fired at you this afternoon were from the same gun, sir.'

'Well, that's something,' Dawlish said. 'Perhaps there aren't swarms of these chaps. What about the gun?'

'Unknown,' Scott answered.

'It can't be!'

'That's what I was saying in effect to the chap from Ballistics, and he didn't think it funny,' the younger man replied. 'He says it is of no known make and has no distinguishing marks. It's very light and made of some kind of unidentified alloy. He thought at first it was a Toro, a neat little Japanese job, but it definitely isn't. He thinks it's manufactured by someone unknown in the small-arms manufacturing field. He's sending it over right away.'

## CHAPTER EIGHT

# TIME BOMB?

DAWLISH said slowly: 'I've heard of home-made guns, guns made by small engineering firms, guns made for a short period and then dropped, but except for the home-made ones these are all on the record. I wonder what we've come up against, Gordon.'

Gordon Scott made no attempt to reply, but it was he who broke the silence a few moments later.

'They're sending Pence back with two cars ahead of him and two cars behind. He should be at the clinic by seven o'clock.'

'It would be nice to think he knows more than he's told me,' said Dawlish. 'Any report from the Staines by-pass?'

'It depends what you mean by a report, sir. Seven people were killed and three are on the danger list in Staines Hospital. Twelve cars were wrecked. The old Austin is a complete write-off – obviously meant to be self-destructive. Other people on the road confirm it was under remote control – at least it had no visible driver. The most likely people to see what happened were those in the following cars, of course, but . . .' Gordon Scott shrugged. 'Whether this one blew up on the collision, or whether there was a timing device, no one knows.'

Dawlish felt a sudden stab of fear.

'Timing device?' He leaned over the desk and picked up the direct line to the Stolen Car Squad, dialled, and waited, tension growing as he tapped his foot on the floor. *Brrr-brrr; brrr-brrr. He couldn't be too late, could he?*

A man said in a very quiet voice: 'Car Squad.'

'This is Dawlish. That M.G.—'

'No M.G., sir,' the speaker interrupted very quietly. 'A new type of engine altogether. We think there may be an explosive device built-in, and we've cleared the place except for a few experts who are dismantling the thing. Have you any reason to suspect a device, sir?'

'Suspicion, yes. Certainty, no. For the love of heaven, be careful.'

'Don't worry about that, sir, none of us wants to be blown to Kingdom Come. I'll report as soon as there's news.'

The man rang off.

Scott was staring, face set, eyes touched with fear.

'I want a car downstairs at once. I'm going over,' Dawlish said. 'Get an army bomb disposal unit over there as soon as you can.' He spun round, banged his knee, rasped: 'Damn this bloody knee!' and limped across to the door. He pulled it open and strode out.

Harris was in the passage.

'Lift,' Dawlish grunted, and the other man hurried to press the button. 'Glad you weren't hurt when you chased that car,' Dawlish went on. 'You could have broken your neck.'

'There's always a risk,' Harris said, as the lift doors opened. 'Are you all right, sir?'

'Bumped my knee. That so-called M.G. wasn't an M.G. It's over at the Stolen Car Department where they think it may have a built-in time bomb. I'm going to see.'

'A car is on standby,' Harris reported. 'Shall I come with you in the car, or follow?'

'Better follow,' Dawlish said. 'And stay outside the garage.'

'If you insist.'

'I do insist,' Dawlish said testily.

What was the matter with him? Why was he so short-tempered and impatient? He was in a constant state of agitation.

Could he be scared?

'Scared as hell,' he muttered under his breath.

If Harris heard, he made no comment.

A police cordon blocked off the approach road to the garage, and over the heads of hundreds of lookers-on was a fire-engine and an ambulance. Firemen in steel helmets and ambulance men in their peaked steel caps stood by. Dawlish's driver approached from another road, but this, too, was chock-a-block. The driver pulled up close to a policeman and Dawlish got out. Near a pile of sandbags outside the wide double doors of the garage stood a bald-headed man with a bony face and the appropriate name of Skeltel; he was the chief inspector in charge of the garage and stolen-car section. Dawlish reached him as a man standing by tugged at his, Skeltel's sleeve, and the bald-headed man looked round.

'Mr. Dawlish – I was told you were on your way.'

They shook hands.

'Anything new?' asked Dawlish.

'An R.A.O.C. lieutenant and a corporal turned up on motor-bikes just now.' Skeltel had a very pleasant voice. 'They've hardly had time to say anything except that it's a new one on them.'

'I'd like to see if it's a new one on me,' Dawlish declared.

'I hope you won't insist, sir,' said Skeltel, looking apologetic. 'The Assistant Commissioner gave strict orders to allow no one in.'

'But he wouldn't mean me.'

'You were specifically named, sir,' said Skeltel, to Dawlish's astonishment. 'We can't afford to lose—'

A man called out from inside the garage: 'Look out!'

As the words came there was a bright flash with a blue tinge, rather like a magnesium flash, and a crack of sound. A dozen men flung themselves down behind the sandbags. People in the crowd surged back and a woman screamed. A man bellowed: 'Here it comes!'

But nothing more came; no explosion, no flash, no smell – and in fact no sound at all until a man spoke with deep satisfaction.

'That was the fuse – we got it disconnected in time ... There's the timing device ... Smallest one I've ever seen. Be careful with that bottle of windscreen fluid. We'll put it in that box of sand and get it loaded.' A moment later he appeared at the open doorway. 'All clear, Inspector. If you will let us get through. Why, hallo, Major Dawlish!'

It was a long time since Dawlish had been called 'Major' or had his hand wrung with greater vigour, and he recognized a one-time sergeant in bomb-disposal, a man who had served with him at the end of the war.

'Hallo, Clarkson.' As the man's face flushed with pleasure at being recognized, he went on: 'A new one on you, you say?'

'Different kind of fuse from any I've ever seen. Linked with the fluid in the windscreen washer which is one of the few conventional parts of the car. All alloy engine – quarter of the size of anything else I've seen. Care to come round and have a peek?'

'Very much,' said Dawlish. 'Wouldn't we, Inspector?'

Inspector Skeltel also looked pleased and Dawlish himself felt happier. Was it because there seemed no danger of an explosion now? Or was it because his hunch that there might be an explosive device here, as on the Austin, had been so quickly vindicated?

The engine was just as tiny as Captain Clarkson had said; smaller than a 150 c.c. motor-engine. It was hard to believe it had driven the mock M.G. at such speed and had had such fierce acceleration.

Clarkson was to take the device to his headquarters and give it a thorough examination. The police-car experts were to work again on the tiny engine. The only comment Skeltel made was that it was like nothing he had ever seen. 'It certainly isn't internal combustion. Shouldn't think it's nuclear energy but there's no way of being sure. Shouldn't worry about radio-activity, though, the driver sits next to it all the time, and he was alive and kicking, wasn't he?'

'Yes,' Dawlish had to admit.

'It could conceivably be driven by electrical impulses from a transistor-type store of electricity, or high-concentrated battery cells, but – well, we'll find out as soon as we can, sir.'

'I'm sure you will.'

'I wonder if you'd come and have a drink in my office,' Skeltel suggested. 'And you ought to get that knee cleaned up a bit, it doesn't look too good.'

He hustled Dawlish into a chair, propped his leg up on a stool, while a youthful-looking St. John Ambulance Brigade man brought in a bowl of warm water, towels and an antiseptic. He sponged and cleaned the knee, then applied a large piece of sticking plaster.

'I've some cloth-patch for that tear, sir. I'll put a piece inside the leg and stick the cloth to it. You'll hardly realize it has been torn, then.' He did the job as he outlined, with a quick and expert touch.

'Excuse me, sir,' Harris said, 'but you're due on the air in less than an hour. Where will you have the interview – here, at your headquarters, or at your home? They'll be outdoor shots, so you can have it where you like.'

'Not home,' Dawlish decided. Then he thought that it might make Felicity happier, and he could not see any harm coming from it. 'Yes, my home!' he changed his mind. 'I can wash and brush up there to look my prettiest!'

Everyone laughed dutifully.

He telephoned Felicity and warned her what to expect, then went with a police car ahead of him and another behind to the office block on the Embankment. A few people, presumably reporters, were watching there, and several threw questions at him.

'I'll answer as many as you like and give you all the information you require both after and during the television and radio show,' he promised. 'But none until it begins. Will you arrange for an informal press conference in the downstairs foyer at my place?' he asked Harris.

'Yes, sir.'

He went up in the elevator alone, not knowing quite what to expect. As the lift stopped, he found two men waiting, one on either side. These were Crime Haters men; he had never known them take better care of him.

'Is anyone with my wife?' he asked.

'No, sir. She had a visitor, a Mrs. Beresford, this afternoon but she left an hour ago.'

'Thank you.' The Beresfords were their oldest friends, it was good that Joan had taken the time and the trouble to come and see Felicity. He unlocked the door with his key, hesitated for a moment and then braced himself. It had been quite a day, and he did not want Felicity to see how much it had taken out of him. He stepped inside.

For a moment, she didn't reply to his: 'Hi there!' and he did not see her, he felt a rush of alarm; but it faded as she came quickly from the bedroom.

'Hallo, darling!' She looked enormously relieved. 'I was afraid you'd be much later – what time is the show?'

'Six o'clock,' he answered.

'Then you've time to relax for half an hour,' she declared. 'Will you have a drink first and then a shower, or——'

'Drink and shower simultaneously,' he said.

56

It was all so pleasant and familiar: the way she actually turned the shower on for him, put towels out, put a whisky and soda close to the shower stall and, while he was under the stinging cold water, put out his clothes. By the time he had dressed he felt invigorated; at five to six he was in the main room, at the long window overlooking London, another drink in his hand, and Felicity by his side.

She had not harassed him with a single question.

'We'll talk after the fun and games,' he promised. 'You'll hear most of the story in questions and answers.'

'Except the things you don't want them to know,' Felicity retorted drily.

Suddenly there was a ring at the front-door bell. It heralded the arrival of the television and radio men. Soon they had set up their microphones and tape recorders and cameras, and the questions came thick and fast.

*Had* he been attacked in Bournemouth?

Yes.

A man called out: 'Have you any idea what this is about, Deputy?' and Dawlish answered as he had the commissioner that afternoon. For the first time he had a chance to look about him, and suddenly saw the last person he had expected to be here: the young and charming girl reporter who had talked to him last night: Sue Somebody-or-other. Day. Sue Day. She had been surprisingly well informed about the Crime Haters.

Close to her – with no one in between – was a small, dark-haired, sharp-featured man. He bore a remarkable resemblance to the prisoner who would not talk.

CHAPTER NINE

A GIRL NAMED SUE

THE session in the apartment was over.

At least sixty reporters were now crowded into the foyer downstairs when Dawlish stepped, quickly, out of the lift.

Harris and two other policemen cleared a path to a small rostrum, put up for the purpose; standing on it, Dawlish towered above everyone. That made him a perfect target for anyone at the edge of the crowd who cared to take a pot shot at him.

Sue Day and her companion were now at one side, the man holding a miniature camera to his eye. Was it a ciné camera, Dawlish asked himself? Or did that tiny lens conceal the barrel of a small automatic pistol?

The same questions came and were answered. They were followed by others.

'Do you have any idea who is behind this, Deputy A.C.?'

'No.'

'Do you think it's been going on for some time?'

'Yes.'

'How long have you known about it?'

'That,' said Dawlish, raising one eyebrow, 'would be telling.'

'Do you think you are close to finding the identity of the criminals?'

'Do you think that's why these attempts are being made on your life?'

'To the first, I hope so. To the second, possibly.'

A man called in a loud aside: 'You're pretty good at evasion, sir.'

'I'm alive,' Dawlish retorted.

There was a general laugh, and for the first time a brief lull in the questions. Dawlish caught Sue's eye. She was looking flushed, which might be because the foyer was very warm. It became her. Against the dark hair and sallow skin of her companion her blonde hair and fair skin showed up vividly.

She called in a clear, rather high-pitched voice:

'Have any other members of the Crime Haters been attacked, do you know?'

'I've heard of none.'

'Does that mean that these acts of hostility are aimed solely at England?'

'It means that England is the centre of activity at the moment,' Dawlish replied. 'The same problem faces other nations – the problem of the brain drain, I mean.'

A man called: 'Not America, surely.'

'Yes, very much America. Most of the major industrial nations are finding it a problem.'

'Do you mean there aren't enough real experts to go round?' asked a man.

'It could be.'

'So everyone is stealing from one another?' Sue's voice was less high-pitched, now; she had overcome her nervousness.

'Possibly,' Dawlish agreed.

'A kind of cannibalism,' she suggested.

'That's one way of putting it!' Dawlish smiled.

By now everyone in the room was looking towards Sue, most of them on tiptoe, to see over the heads of the crowd. Several photographers took pictures of her. She seemed oblivious of the attention she was getting and intent only on Dawlish.

'Or industrial anarchy on a global scale,' a balding, middle-aged man suggested. 'Don't you think the time has come to stop this kind of cut-throat competition, Mr. Dawlish?'

'Personally, yes, but as a policeman I have no political opinions about cases I'm working on. Industrial anarchy or industrial cannibalism isn't exactly new, and as far as I know there's no law against it. But once anyone – individual, corporation or state – begins to break existing laws, then in I come, with both feet. I've been in touch with most of the delegates to the International Police Conference, and we may have a meeting here in London or in some other major industrial city before long. And *that*,' added Dawlish, clapping his hands together resonantly, 'has to be everything for now.'

Half a dozen more questions came, simultaneously, but he made no attempt to answer them. He bent his head to Harris who stood just behind him.

'Have the cannibal girl followed,' he whispered. 'I want a minute-by-minute report.'

'It's been arranged,' Harris said. 'Less because of what she said than because of the man she was with.' He was looking into the foyer, Dawlish's back was towards it. 'They're coming towards you, sir.'

'I'll talk to them,' said Dawlish. He half-turned, saw two other reporters waiting, old acquaintances who wanted no

59

more than to show their special relationship. Then Dawlish turned again and his eyes widened as if in surprise at sight of Sue Day.

'Hallo, hallo,' he boomed. 'Having a day away from the briny, Miss Cannibal?'

She laughed easily.

'That's *one* word that will hit all the newspapers,' she declared. 'So will industrial anarchy.' She was smiling as if quietly pleased with herself. 'My paper gave me a special assignment after what happened last night – they are becoming conscious of the big wide world after all.' There was a curious mixture of naiveté and sophistication about her, although the overall impression she made was still of a very young woman.

Throughout these exchanges her companion stood by, making no attempt to intrude. Now, she glanced at him and he inclined his head in a little bow.

'Mr. Dawlish, I would like to introduce a friend of mine,' she said. 'Mr. Sorio.' The man's dark eyes were remarkably like those of the prisoner, and their gaze was very direct. Challenging? Was this a chance meeting or had he deliberately engineered it, through the girl?

'Mr. Sorio?' Dawlish said, offering his hand.

'I am very glad to meet you.' Sorio's hand was small, and dwarfed in Dawlish's, but it was also very firm; and, surprisingly, chill. 'I have known of you for a long time, Mr. Dawlish, and I am going to ask if you would allow me a very great favour.'

'And that is?' asked Dawlish pleasantly.

He saw the badge in the man's lapel buttonhole. It was of gold, a quite beautifully-made trumpet. A shock ran through him, for he remembered seeing a similar badge in young Osgood's buttonhole. For a moment it seemed to him that he could still hear the haunting note of the trumpet at the house in Bournemouth.

Dawlish was aware of the girl's glance, watchful and intent, as if she were willing him to do what Sorio asked. The foyer was empty now but for Harris and some other policemen; the snort of cars starting outside seemed never-ending.

'To grant me an interview for a special article for my newspaper,' Sorio said.

'I would need to know what newspaper,' said Dawlish.

'It is a small one but most unique,' Sorio told him, and he slid his hand inside his jacket. It was exactly the movement that a man would make when going for a gun in a shoulder holster, and Dawlish flexed his right arm, to strike if a gun appeared. But all the man brought out was a thin sheaf of papers. He unfolded them, revealing eight pages of very fine rice paper. The printing was clearly marked, the form that of a weekly review, such as the *Spectator* or the *Economist*. There was a small front-page heading, which read:

*The Global Trumpet*
*The Newspaper which Believes in One World*

The motif, at one side, was a trumpet the size of the young man's lapel badge.

Dawlish glanced at the headlines.

'And what makes it unique?'

'It is published simultaneously in twenty-four languages and in twenty-four different parts of the world,' answered Sorio. 'The purpose is a clarion cry for all people to listen. Its articles are all directed to one end – to show how the interests of all people are, fundamentally, the same and interdependent. In art, or—'

'And how would you treat an article on me?' asked Dawlish.

'Very simply, sir. I would show that the problem of crime and the investigation of crime, the search for criminals – all of these and allied matters are similar in most countries. And with your permission I would say that you were among the first to recognize this fact.'

Dawlish turned to Sue and asked, his eyes merry: 'Did you tell him this?'

'Miss Day is a constant source of valuable information,' said Sorio, earnestly.

Dawlish gave a dry smile.

'You shouldn't believe everything she tells you. You might get many disappointments. If you will telephone Chief Inspector Gordon Scott at the office he will arrange a fifteen-minute interview one day next week. That will be as long as I can spare, I'm afraid.'

The dark eyes lit up.

'You are very good,' breathed Sorio.

'Bless you,' said Sue Day, and stretching up on tiptoe, she kissed Dawlish on the cheek. Ignoring Harris's look of astonishment, she then put a hand on Sorio's arm and led him across the foyer. Neither of them looked round again, but Dawlish, striding to the door, saw them getting into an M.G. which looked identical with the one on which there had been a timing device set for an explosion.

They went off together; Sorio at the wheel.

'Pat,' said Felicity.

'Sweetheart,' responded Dawlish, vaguely.

'Come back.'

'Come back from – oh. Have I been away for long?'

'Most of the time through dinner.'

'And it was such a nice dinner,' Dawlish mourned.

'I don't for a moment think you know what it tasted like.'

'Nonsense! I haven't tasted a better filet mignon for months!'

'It was boned neck of lamb.'

'Oh, darling! Couldn't have been!'

'Pat,' Felicity said again, 'listen to me. Really listen. Would you rather I went away for a few days?'

Dawlish didn't answer.

There had been a time when he hated the thought of exposing Felicity to danger; and in one way he still hated it. But the years had simply accustomed them both to such a situation: if they were to live together in their marriage, which was so much happier than many, then sometimes they had to share a risk. This had become less important than being separated for long periods; and periods of separation were dwarfed by those briefer ones when Dawlish needed to concentrate on the work in hand so much that he hardly realized she was with him; worse, when he had to force his mind away from the work and on to her.

They had long ago agreed that each would tell the truth about such a situation; and now he smiled at her, and said simply:

'Where would you go?'

'Joan is taking the children for a few days to Cornwall, and Ted's going to France on a business trip. I could go with Joan—'

'Or Ted!'

'Ass!'

'Sorry, dear. Have you seen Kathy lately?'

'Last week, just before we left,' Felicity replied. 'She's exactly like one of their own children. I think she always will be.'

Kathy was the child of a man who had been murdered; a child whose life Dawlish had helped to save and who had been adopted by their friends the Beresfords. That had been a case when for a day Felicity had been in acute danger.

'Good,' he said. 'No.'

'No what?'

'I wouldn't like you to go away. Apart from wanting to talk this over with you, and you *were* in it from the beginning, there's something I think you can do. Remember Sue Day?'

'The Bournemouth newspaperwoman?'

'She was downstairs with a man remarkably like the johnny who shot at me on the cliff last night. He represents a newspaper called the *Global Trumpet*. She knows a remarkable lot about the Crime Haters and me. She's had a special assignment for this job, and will be in London for a few days. I can't be sure whether she is what she seemed to be—'

'I can tell you this,' said Felicity stoutly, 'she's much tougher than she looks.'

'Feminine intuition?' asked Dawlish.

Felicity shrugged. 'You can call it that. What do you want me to do?'

'Stand by, and if the chance arises, find out what you can about her. Good girl or bad girl, my paper right or wrong, anything you can. Sweetheart.' Dawlish leaned forward. 'Tell me if you hate the idea and would rather go away.'

'I'd rather stay here,' Felicity declared. 'It's a prop to my ego to be wanted. I'm too conceited – or not conceited enough – to resist it. Yes, I *do* know I shall be on my own a great deal before this is over, and I do know you may have to go to the other ends of the earth. Are you going to the office tonight?'

'Yes,' Dawlish answered, 'And I ought to be on my way.'

Gordon Scott, looking red and weary about the eyes said: 'Glad to see you, sir,' as Dawlish entered.

'What's come in?' asked Dawlish.

'Pence is at the clinic,' answered Scott. 'He's maintaining his improvement. He actually sent a message saying he would like to see you as soon as possible.'

'Another glutton for punishment. And?'

'The gun has arrived from Ballistics.' Scott handed over the automatic wrapped in a plastic container. Dawlish unpacked it thoughtfully. It was very light and cold. In a way it reminded him of Sorio's hand. Idiotic thought! 'They still don't recognize it, and they've had it examined by Industrial Research. It's definitely a metal alloy of some kind, but the actual basic metal isn't known'

'Not plastic?'

'The experts say no.' Scott gulped. 'Believe it or not, sir, but the bullets are made of the same alloy. So is the engine of the car that didn't blow up. Whoever is behind this affair has discovered a metallic alloy which will stand up to a great deal of rough treatment. Some small pieces of the metal were found in the wrecked engine of the Austin, the one that so nearly got you,' went on Scott. 'The ordinary metal had been fused by the heat, the engine misshapen and useless, but this alloy doesn't appear to have been affected. So it can stand extremely high temperatures.'

'Yes,' Dawlish agreed, heavily. 'Extreme heat and great pressure.' He sat down at his desk and pulled a file towards him: the one marked C2. A glance told him that by now everyone to whom he had sent the message had replied.

On top was a note in Gordon Scott's bold handwriting: it said:

100% response, and 100% anxiety about the brain drain. This could be one firm but it doesn't look like any one nation.

## CHAPTER TEN

# 100%

ON the second sheet Dawlish found a summary of the replies from all over the world. In it, Gordon Scott's handwriting became very ragged and some of the numerals were hard to read. But its message was clear enough. Every one of the nations and the large aeronautical firms questioned by the Crime Haters complained of their best men being lured away by large salaries, often by additional, substantial sums.

The United States remained on the top of the list of nations blamed as the chief offender; and it was also at the top of the list of complainants. Great Britain was fifth as an offender, second as a sufferer, but after the United States there was little difference in the actual figures for Great Britain, Germany, France, Japan and Italy. Dawlish flipped over the pages, soaking up the information and coming suddenly and unexpectedly on another summary – placed at the back instead of the front.

Forty-seven nations or corporations reported the accidental death of brilliant research workers; and twenty-one such men were missing. Three American and one Japanese corporation said there was reason to believe that a man who had died 'by accident' had refused an offer to go to an overseas company.

Dawlish pushed his chair back, and whistled only just above his breath. Then he drew a notepad close and picked up a pencil.

*Urgent request to all delegates*

Now vital to find out if individuals who refused to leave their present employment and afterwards died by accident, or are missing, could have been victims of foul play. Stop. Equally vital to find out if any one company, country or corporation anywhere, could be responsible

for the bribing and/or inducements. Stop. Some indications in England of a new light-weight alloy of exceptional toughness being used for guns, car engines, bomb devices. Stop. Further indications of the existence of a form of power not clearly identified – an engine less than a quarter of the size and an eighth of the weight of a conventional internal combustion engine undoubtedly exists. Stop. These things could point to breakthroughs in metallurgy, odourless power emissions, substantial reduction in noise. Stop. Strongly recommend urgent inquiries into all these fields and a meeting in London or New York within ten days. Stop. One of the people involved who either does not understand, or will not speak, any of the major languages appears to have some unusual physical aspects – small of stature, lean, upright, sharp-featured, dark-eyed, dark hair worn without a parting, powerful grip, great physical courage. Stop. Two such men known. Stop. One is known to represent small circulation newspaper published in a variety of languages under the title of the *Global Trumpet*. A small trumpet is worn as a lapel badge. Stop. Recommend immediate inquiry into *G.T.* for possible later use. Stop. Recommend this whole matter be now treated as an emergency. Reports please to me here in London.
Message ends.

He put this aside for a moment as Scott, who had been in the next office, came in with some papers in his hand.

'Anything new?' asked Dawlish.

'Seven different metallurgical laboratories have now analysed the contents of the alloy and none is able positively to identify,' answered Scott. 'Copper is the only common constituent.'

'Any report from the men following the girl Day and the man Sorio?' asked Dawlish.

'Nothing, yet,' Scott replied.

'If anything comes in let me know at the clinic,' Dawlish said. 'I'm going to talk to Pence.'

'There is one other thing, sir,' said Scott, and when Dawlish simply waited, he went on: 'The first of the television newscasts has been made, and several radio broadcasts. Calls are beginning to reach Scotland Yard from a great variety of companies complaining that they've been losing research workers to unfair competition.'

'They can't think it's new,' Dawlish said drily. 'But every one wants checking, in case we find another Ryall affair. Pence really started something, didn't he?'

Scott laughed.

The clinic was in fact an ordinary clinic but it was also a nursing and convalescent home, and even a private hotel and guest house. One of several similar establishments run either by or for the police, it was strongly guarded, and wounded or sick police officers as well as wounded or sick criminals were often there at the same time, unknown to each other. The clinic itself was in St. John's Wood, not far from Swiss Cottage, and what looked like four three-storey Victorian houses had been knocked into one; from the outside it looked small; inside there was room for forty guests or patients.

Policemen guarded the place, back and front, night and day.

As Dawlish drew up in a police car with a chauffeur, he saw two groups of workers, one at electricity mains and one at water mains; these would be extra guards because of Pence.

Inside, the woodwork was painted a gloss-finished white, too bright for Dawlish, but there could be no doubt of the cleanliness. A porter took him to the matron, a small woman with greying hair; she was an old acquaintance of Dawlish.

'I saw the television broadcast an hour ago,' she said. 'I must tell you that you seem born to the medium, Mr. Dawlish!'

'Born to talk too much,' Dawlish replied. 'Well, how's my patient?'

'A very lucky and a very impatient one,' the matron told him. 'Now there *is* a man who wants to talk too much. He won't stop asking for you.'

'Then it's time I went to see him,' Dawlish declared.

Ex-Chief Inspector Hugo Pence was sitting back on highly stacked pillows in a small, white-furnished room. A plain-clothes officer sat with him. The radio was on.

'Mr. Pence – ' began the matron.

'*Ssshhh!*' breathed Pence, without looking round.

67

Then Dawlish recognized his own voice over the radio and knew why the injured man was so intent. He nodded towards the door, and first the matron and then the policeman went out. The recording was in its final sentences, and Dawlish heard himself say:

'Anyone who can give us the slightest help should get in touch with—'

Pence turned his head, then started as if he could not believe his eyes. There was sweat on his forehead and his upper lip, the tension of listening had obviously been grave indeed. Dawlish went over and shook hands.

'Hallo, Pence,' he said. 'I'm glad you're no worse.'

'I'm glad you're as good as ever,' Pence said. He spoke with difficulty. There was a bandage round his neck, and a patch on his left temple. 'It would never have occurred to me to go into the attack like that.'

'If we make the other side realize that we've already told the world, they won't waste any more time trying to prevent us talking,' Dawlish said. He pulled up a chair, noticing the other's colour was good and that the deep-set eyes did not look anything like as tired as they had done on the previous night. 'I'm told you want to see me.'

'They just wouldn't let me talk to you and nearly drove me mad saying I had to rest. *I* know whether I'm fit or not. They wouldn't tell me a thing, but I'd make a guess that my room at the pub in Wilbury was ransacked.'

'Right in one,' said Dawlish. 'Not a single document was left.'

To his astonishment, Pence actually burst out laughing, only to stop abruptly and put his hand to his neck; obviously the outburst had hurt. But laughter was soon back in his eyes, and he said huskily:

'I wonder what made the idiots think I'd leave anything that mattered there.'

'Nice work! What about your office at Astrid's?'

'Was that raided?'

'We haven't been told so, but it's always closely guarded.'

'That's true enough,' agreed Pence. 'Well, they wouldn't have had any luck there either, sir. I've got a complete record of all I've done on the case, with a cross-file index.' So Gordon Scott had been right about him. 'But I didn't leave it about where anyone could find it.'

'Nice work,' repeated Dawlish. 'Where did you leave it?'

'With a friend at Scotland Yard,' Pence told him. 'Superintendent Wallace, sir. I left it with him and asked him to let you have it if anything happened to me, and the A.C. over at the Yard if anything happened to you.'

'Well, well,' Dawlish said. 'The stick-in-the-mud Hugo Pence!'

'You can't tell what goes on in a man's mind by an assessment of his outside,' Pence declared with a shrug. 'It all sounds a bit cloak-and-dagger I grant you, but then it was a cloak-and-dagger situation. If I was right, then poor Ryall and his family had been cold-bloodedly murdered simply because Ryall wouldn't go off and do what this man Polkov wanted. So I dug deep, sir – I really dug deep.'

'What did you find?' asked Dawlish.

'One hundred and seven men in the British aeronautical and motor-research industry have been approached. Sixty-one moved away from their jobs. Of the others, four died – two with their families in car crashes, one in a fire at a hotel where he was staying. The others stayed put and nothing happened to them. Presumably they weren't important enough in the scheme of things.' Pence stopped, but obviously hadn't finished, and Dawlish waited, watching the dark, deep-set eyes which now seemed to burn.

'Care to make a guess at what comes next, sir?' asked Pence.

'If it won't disappoint you if I'm right.'

'I'd be very glad, sir.'

'I'll try,' Dawlish said; sliding back in his chair and thrusting his long legs forward. He looked not only comfortable, but as if he hadn't a care in the world. 'Sunk without trace.'

'You mean – vanished, sir?'

'Yes. You haven't been able to find out whether they are still in England, or if they left, how and when, and you haven't the faintest idea where they are.'

Hugo Pence hitched himself higher on his pillows, his gaze fixed unwaveringly on Dawlish.

'You are absolutely right. Every one disappeared. Some took their families, some didn't say a word to wives or families but just walked out. I can give you chapter and verse for every one, sir, in that cross-index system I told you about. Never worked so hard in my life. Got a lot of help from local police forces and the Yard, of course, relied on the old pal appeal—'

'Or the one-time boss appeal,' Dawlish replied drily. 'It sounds magnificent. I'll try to succeed where you failed, and I'll make it an official inquiry. Where can I get this file?'

'Oh, Wallace will let you have his, on request,' Pence declared.

'Good. One other thing, Pence. This chap Polkov you came across. Did he wear any kind of identification – a ring, or lapel badge, or tie-pin, for instance?'

Pence knitted his brows in an obvious effort to remember, and was silent for some time. Then he said:

'Yes, sir – he wore a trumpet lapel badge. I didn't see any significance in it but I'm sure it was there.' Pence paused again before going on: 'A very small one, sir, which looked as if it was made of gold.'

It was Saturday night, never the best time for record and desk work at New Scotland Yard. But within three hours official requests were out to all police forces covering areas from which the research workers had disappeared. And special information was asked about anyone known to wear a trumpet lapel badge, while the offices of the *Global Trumpet* were to be located and placed under surveillance.

A list of missing research workers with names and photographs was on its way to the delegates of the Crime Haters.

Dawlish, back in his office, did a quick calculation. If sixty-one such men had disappeared from England it was safe, when estimating, to assume that at least twenty had disappeared from each of the countries or organizations which had complained of the brain drain. There were sixty-eight such units, which meant upwards of one thousand four hundred men.

'It's more than a team of research workers, it's a labour force,' Dawlish said to Gordon Scott.

'And this could be only the beginning, sir. I wonder what the hell is going on?'

'Whatever it is, Pence can cross-index it,' Dawlish said,

half-seriously. 'Is there any word from Harris or anyone who was following Sue Day and Sorio?'

'The couple had dinner together,' Gordon answered. 'Then they went on to a night club. I've checked this *Global* newspaper, and it seems genuine enough, all high-minded do-gooding pie-in-the-sky stuff.'

'Hard days for idealists,' Dawlish remarked drily. 'Well! I'm going home. It's time you did, too.' He pushed back his chair, yawned, stretched, and then the outside telephone on his desk rang. He was momentarily tempted to turn to the door, but slowly he stretched out his hand and plucked up the receiver.

'Dawlish,' he announced.

'This – this is Harris, sir,' said a man who was so obviously agitated that Dawlish motioned Scott to an extension. 'The – the place is blazing like an inferno, sir. An inferno.'

'What place do you mean, Sergeant?'

'The club, sir. It's – it's an absolute inferno. I don't see how anybody can get out.'

'*Which club?*' demanded Dawlish sharply. 'And where is it?'

'The one Sue Day and the man went to, sir. The – the Cloven Hoof. It's in Soho, in Dean Street. There was an explosion and it caught fire.'

As the man stopped speaking, Dawlish heard the faint clanging of a fire-engine bell and the wail of police and ambulance sirens over the telephone.

Sue Day had not really wanted to go to the Cloven Hoof.

She had been busy since the early hours, as well as late to bed the night before. She had enjoyed dinner with Sorio, who intrigued her with his precise manner and careful English, with his burning enthusiasm for his newspaper and its ideals; but she had been very tired, and would gladly have gone straight to her hotel after dinner.

'Just dance for a little while,' he had urged her.

'But I'm not dressed for dancing.'

'It is simply a small club, frequented by tourists, and no one will be dressed better than you. Certainly none will look more beautiful,' he had added with simple gallantry. 'It will be both a pleasure and an honour to dance with you.'

Her resistance had crumpled.

The Cloven Hoof proved a tawdry place, but the band was good. There was a quite exceptional trumpet player, who was darker-skinned than the other players. Dancing was in Sue's blood, and it was obvious that Sorio loved dancing, too. Slowly she forgot her tiredness; no doubt three gin and Italians in quick succession helped her. She might have stayed on the floor much longer than she had but for a shoulder strap, which snapped.

'Damn!' she exclaimed. 'Sorio, I'll have to go and do some running repairs. I won't be long.'

The powder room was down a narrow staircase, and there was hardly room for two people at the tiny dressing-table with its garish, over-bright lights, and only one stool. She was sitting with her dress falling from her shoulder, looking exasperatedly at the torn strap, when the explosion came. A second later there was a rumbling sound above, as if the whole of the building was falling on top of her.

CHAPTER ELEVEN

## DEATH ABOVE

ONE moment before, there had been lively music, a dozen couples on the dance floor, a few hostesses at the bar, men drinking more than was good for them. Around the walls couples were sitting at small tables. The band of four long-haired youths and a slip of a girl with a startlingly big bosom were playing as if they were really enjoying themselves.

Sorio sat at the table by himself, very still, watching the door through which Sue had gone. There was a strange, half-fearful expression on his face. One man at the bar moved from his stool and came towards him.

'It is time to leave,' he said abruptly. He was very short, and not unlike Sorio himself.

'I am not coming,' Sorio responded.

'The girl cannot be so important to you,' argued the man from the bar.

'Important enough,' answered Sorio. 'I am not coming.'

The man stared at him for at least thirty seconds, then turned away, without any change of expression. He moved back to the bar and on to the doorway marked *Exit*: there was still another flight of stairs up to street level. He disappeared behind the bead curtains at the doorway, ran up the staircase, passed the little pay-box, and walked briskly to the end of the street.

He had just turned the corner when the explosion came.

In the Cloven Hoof itself there was the band and the few necking couples and a drunk pawing one of the hostesses. The explosion came from the doorway – a flash, a roar, a blast of hot air, and then a raging fire which spread with terrifying speed across the entrance. After the moment of shock, when the music stopped and no one moved, a man bellowed: '*Fire!*' and a girl screamed. One of the bandsmen, his fuzzy hair a halo in the reflected light, picked up the girl singer and leapt off the platform. Covering his face with his coat, he lunged forward to the door; they disappeared and there was no way of telling whether they reached the staircase. Another man, dragging a screaming girl, staggered within a yard of the exit: then his hair caught alight, turning him into a flaming torch. Together they pitched forward.

The flames devoured them.

The flames devoured everyone.

But they did not travel downwards.

The hot, stinking air did; and the noise, the sound of screaming and the sound of roaring, but not the actual flames.

Sue moved to the door of the dressing-room. She saw the red glow at the top of the stairs and heard the roar of the flames. She turned back. Her eyes ran desperately over the walls, but there was no window, only an air shaft. She knew this was the only possible hope of attracting attention, and she called through it:

'Help! Help!'

Only a shivering kind of echo came back to her.

She went out to the staircase, but now there were flames everywhere and the stench of fire and burning flesh. The heat made her gasp. As she stood there, something fell with a roar and the top of the stairway was blocked with burning debris, part of the walls and part of the ceiling. A burning chair fell, step by step, flaming pieces breaking off and sending forth showers of sparks. She turned away desperately, went back to the cubicle, and called again into the grille:

'Help! Help!'

But she did not think she had any chance of being heard.

The shaft ran up to a small courtyard. Electric and gas meters and telephone cables were here, in a kind of pit reached by a narrow alley between two buildings. Piles of newspapers and old rags filled this pit, and tramps slept there as if by right.

One was sleeping there when the explosion came.

He was half-drunk and very bleary, but the explosion roused him. So far neither heat nor flame had reached this place, and there was no sign of danger. Muttering to himself, he settled back on his bed of newspapers and lay breathing stertorously. Into his consciousness there came a sound he had not heard before. It was like a woman crying from a long way off:

'Help! Help!'

He turned over, trying to keep the sound out of his ears, but it was just as plain from the other side:

'Help! Help!'

'Shut up, can't you?' he muttered. 'Shut up!'

Soon, other sounds intruded: of sirens and a fire engine bell, all quite near. There was still no sign of fire here, unless a faint red glow in the sky above the pit was from the fire. More likely neon lights, he told himself. None of my business, anyway. He tried to settle down again but the noises grew louder, and through them all came the cry:

'Help! Help!'

At long, long last, he got to his feet, went along the passage, found people in great crowds at the right-hand corner and police keeping them back. There was an excited hum of talk, and the word fire was repeated over and over again.

'Fire! Fire!'

'Help! Help!'

He pushed his way into the crowd, but he was old and weak. Although he could see a policeman he had no hope of making himself heard. Now, frustrated, the echo of that cry for help seemed stronger and his will to respond much greater.

'I've got to see a copper,' he began to say. 'Got to see a copper. Let me through. I've got to see a copper.'

It took him five minutes but he managed to reach the front, where wooden barricades had been put across the roadway, guarded by three policemen in uniform. He went up to one of them, who seemed no more than a boy, and who turned and looked at him, half-smiling.

'Hallo, Dad,' he said. 'What's your trouble?'

'There's someone calling for help,' the tramp declared. 'It started just after the explosion. There's someone asking for help.'

'You don't mean you think this is a way of free-loading, do you?' asked the policeman.

'If you don't believe me, come and listen. It's a woman, I should say. Keeps calling "Help, help". If you don't believe me, come and listen.'

'I'll tell you what I will do,' said the policeman. 'I'll take you to see the sergeant.' He gripped the frail arm and led the tramp away, to a roar of laughter and a burst of applause.

Ten minutes later a sergeant of police and a Fire Service Officer were in the tiny pit, listening to the cry which came less frequently now, and with much less strength.

'Help . . . help . . .'


When Dawlish reached Dean Street the crowd had been cleared from all the approaches and only fire engines, ambulances and police cars were near the fire. Shops and apartments above them had been evacuated and hoses were being played on all adjoining buildings to the group of three which had suffered the brunt of the explosion.

The fire was still burning fiercely as he got out of the police car. Harris turned towards him.

'Anyone rescued?' Dawlish asked.

'I've just heard that someone may be alive,' Harris explained the tramp's story. 'Firemen are round in the alley now, sir. Apart from that it was – well, a hundred per cent.'

'Were Sue Day and the man Sorio still there?'

'Yes,' answered Harris. 'One odd thing though, sir. A man

very like Sorio was seen leaving the club a minute before the explosion.'

'Was he followed?' demanded Dawlish.

'Yes, sir. But no report has come in yet. Not that we've had much time to check.'

'Where was the man following him to report?'

'Information Room, sir.'

'Check at once from my car,' ordered Dawlish. He turned to a Divisional policeman standing near. 'Can you take me to this alley?'

'Yes, sir.'

Harris went off in one direction, Dawlish and his guide in another. Dawlish had a feeling of irritation but wasn't really sure it was justified. Harris so often seemed to him to do the wrong thing. He should not have needed telling that his priority was to trail the man who resembled Sorio. He did not seem to act with the precision expected of a trained policeman. Even when he had telephoned news of the fire he had seemed over-involved.

On one side of the road hundreds of sightseers were pressing against barriers; on the other was a small fire tender, some police and firemen. As Dawlish and the Divisional man arrived, a fireman wearing a steel helmet came out of a narrow passage, and called to another standing by the entrance:

'There's someone alive, all right.'

'Where?'

'Down in the lav,' the other replied. 'There's a call for help coming up through the ventilator shaft.'

'How big is the shaft?' asked the man by the alley.

'Big enough – eighteen inches by eighteen, I'd say. If we get the grille off and then lower someone down at the end of the rope we ought to be able to bring her up.'

*Her*, thought Dawlish, tensely.

'We'll fix it,' the second fireman said.

'Better get a move on,' the first one replied. 'The cries are getting fainter, and I can smell smoke enough to choke anyone coming out of the shaft.'

There was no way of even guessing whether by freak of chance the woman was Sue Day.

Sue felt the pressure at her eyes and nose, her mouth,

even her ears. The smoke made her cough and choke, weakly. Now and again she called 'help' but it was little more than a sigh and no one could possibly hear it. She had closed the door and was leaning against the wall, so that her face was as near the ventilation shaft as she could be. But now there seemed no clear air at the shaft, it was fouled with the evil-smelling smoke.

And it was dark: pitch dark.

Now and again, when she closd her eyes, there was a fiery red light against her eyelids: remembered light from the top of the narrow stairs. *Fire.*

'Help . . . help.'

A white light shone on her eyes. She opened but closed them again immediately, because the light dazzled her. *White light.* She thought she heard a man talking, but that was absurd. She was drifting: drifting. '*Be all right, don't you worry.*' It was a man's voice. '*Have you out in a brace of shakes.*' It *was* a man's voice! She opened her eyes again. The light was not so bright now, more diffused, and she saw that it shone on a wall, and a man who seemed to be suspended in mid-air. He was making movements with his hands. She heard little, metallic sounds. '*Take it easy, just take it easy. Soon have this grille off.*' She closed her eyes and listened to him vaguely, mistily aware of hands at her shoulders. '*Just putting a rope round your waist, we're going to haul you up, have you out of this in a brace of shakes.*'

'*Up!*' the voice cried again. 'They'll lift, I'll push, you don't do a thing. *Up.*'

'Ready down there?' A voice sounded a long way above.

'All ready. *Up!*'

She felt a tug at the harness, and then suddenly realized that she was suspended in the shaft. It was small, her shoulders and hands brushed against the sides.

'*Up!*'

Slowly, slowly, they pulled her upwards.

Slowly, slowly, Dawlish saw the top of the head become the forehead and the top half of the face; at first he could not believe the truth but soon he had to: this *was* Sue Day. She looked very pale and her eyes were closed, she might be badly hurt, might even be dead from suffocation.

No! She opened her eyes, looked around blankly, and closed them again.

Ten minutes later she was in an ambulance, with a doctor and Dawlish. The doctor used his stethoscope, felt her pulse, put a light close to her eyes and then into her mouth. Dawlish waited in a frenzy of impatience.

At last, the doctor said: 'I can find nothing wrong that a little rest won't cure. Constitutionally I'd say she's a very healthy young woman.'

'What I'd like to do is take her to my home – where my wife will look after her.'

'I can't see any reason why not,' the doctor declared. 'Provided you make sure she rests. A soothing linctus for her throat wouldn't do any harm, it is a little inflamed from the smoke and heat.'

'I can get something even if we've nothing at home,' said Dawlish. 'Tell the driver where to go, will you?'

They pulled up outside the big office block at about one o'clock. Though still dazed and shaken, Sue was able to step out of the ambulance. Dawlish helped her across the foyer and into the lift. Police were on duty everywhere, and when he got up to the penthouse floor, several others were on guard. No one was taking the slightest chance.

Then his own front door was opened by Harris, the last man he had expected to see.

CHAPTER TWELVE

SUCCESS REPORT

Just behind Harris was Felicity; and behind Felicity was Gordon Scott.

'Sue,' Dawlish said, 'this is my wife, Felicity. She'll look after you – and you'll be all right now. If you tell her all you can we won't need to worry you with questions afterwards.'

Felicity put an arm protectively round the girl and led the way towards the spare room.

'We'll get you a warm shower, and then . . .'

Dawlish closed the door behind them quietly.

He did not go immediately to the big room where he would find Scott and Harris, for he needed a few minutes to collect his thoughts and to decide what attitude to take with Harris. Had Gordon Scott brought the man here or had he come on his own? He went into the kitchen and poured a glass of milk and ate some biscuits. He felt relaxed in one way, very tense in another; it would have robbed him of all relaxation had Sue died in the fire. He wondered how soon she would be able to talk sensibly. Shock could sometimes have a long-lasting effect.

Conscientiously washing and putting away his empty glass, he moved on to the big room. Both the others were standing by the window, looking out. Scott heard him and turned round. He had a tankard in his hand; so had Harris. It was surprising how the colouring of these two matched; but standing together there was no other resemblance.

'Hallo, sir,' Scott said. 'We arrived only five minutes ahead of you.'

'With results?' asked Dawlish.

'Yes, sir,' said Harris. 'Information had reports on that man I saw leave the Cloven Hoof, and we know where he is. We haven't taken any action – thought it best to consult you, first.'

'Where is he?'

'At a house in Carpenter Street, Kensington,' Harris answered. 'It stands in its own grounds and has a rather odd name – Trumpet House. There were a number of musical instruments in one of the rooms. As if bands play there. We haven't had anyone too close yet, in case we're seen.'

'How do you know about the musical instruments?' asked Dawlish.

'Division told us,' said Harris.

'Did Division tell you who owns the house? Or lives in it?'

'They're checking, sir,' Harris answered him, 'and meanwhile Division is watching and guarding the place.'

Dawlish said slowly: 'It could be the offices of the *Global Trumpet*. We need to watch from a distance and follow whoever comes out and check on whoever goes in. We need men at the windows of houses opposite, on roofs, anywhere they can see without being seen. Fix it, Gordon. No.' He moved towards a telephone. 'I think we'll work on this one from the top.' He dialled a number and was answered by a man with a brisk voice:

'Sir Arthur Winthrop.'

'Sir Arthur . . .' Dawlish began, and when Winthrop recognized his voice, described the place and everything he wanted, and then went on: 'It might be a good idea to get military help on this, sir – that's why I've approached you in person.'

'I will arrange it,' promised Winthrop. 'Don't hesitate to get in touch with me direct on anything connnected with this affair.'

'Believe me I won't, sir,' Dawlish said.

He replaced the receiver as the commissioner rang off, and moved towards the two men. Harris was looking very red about the eyes, and his face was drawn.

Dawlish said abruptly: 'When did you last have some sleep?'

Harris gave a wry smile. 'Well . . .'

'Then go and get a good night now,' Dawlish ordered. 'The chief inspector will assign someone else to look after me in the morning.'

'Thank you, sir.' Harris put his tankard down, and added: 'And please thank your wife for the beer. It was most welcome.'

'Splendid,' said Dawlish mechanically, and saw the man to the door.

Closing it, he turned to Scott, who was walking to the window, and frowning. Dawlish joined him and he pointed to a red glow in the middle of the dense mass of buildings: there was no doubt this was the Soho fire. They stood rigid for a few moments, before Dawlish said:

'They're utterly ruthless, Gordon.'

'The really bad ones usually are,' Scott retorted.

'The wholly evil and the truly fanatical.'

'Fanatical?' Scott echoed.

'Doesn't it seem that way to you?' asked Dawlish. 'Kill a dozen or a hundred to kill one. The main question we have to ask and answer is whether that fire was started to kill Sue Day.' He had briefed Scott about the girl, and Scott would be quick to see the significance of the question.

He exclaimed: 'If you think that's even half-possible, sir, you should get her away from here!'

'If they know she's here,' Dawlish replied.

'They would only have to have the place watched to know it,' Scott said, and then he added in a tone of exasperation: 'You are the most astonishing man for asking for trouble – sir.'

'Yes, aren't I?' agreed Dawlish. 'Gordon . . .'

'Sir?'

'What do you know about Harris?'

'Very little really. He was seconded from the Yard two months ago when we needed four new men, and had good qualifications. He seems very keen, as I said.'

'Yes,' Dawlish said. 'Eager, ingenuous, very prone to make elementary mistakes. Before he's assigned to this or any other job again I'd like to have his record checked, and go over some details with the Yard. Give him some routine work tomorrow.'

Scott looked as if he wanted to exclaim: 'You can't really suspect Harris of being disloyal!' but Dawlish's expression silenced him except for a quiet:

'Very good, sir.'

'And get some sleep,' Dawlish ordered.

He saw Scott out, feeling the disquiet which he had felt so often in this affair without being able to explain or to understand it. He went to the long couch and stretched out on it, picked up the evening paper and saw his own photograph and a good account of what had happened at Bournemouth, ran through every stage of the affair in his mind as closely as he could, and found only one good aspect: that of Hugo Pence and his cross-indexes. If ever a man had a card-index, it was Pence.

He was half-listening to Pence's remembered voice when Felicity entered the room, looking very tall and attractive in a pale green housecoat.

'She's much better,' she announced, 'and I'm sure she'll talk freely, but I don't think she knows very much, Pat – except about the Crime Haters. Will you talk to her now?'

Felicity had worked miracles.

Sue Day was sitting up in bed, pillows stacked behind

her, wearing a filmy nightdress and dressing-jacket. Her fair hair, brushed back, gave her a look of appeal and youthfulness. By her side was a tray of coffee, and the evening newspapers.

Felicity had placed a large armchair at the foot of the bed for Dawlish; and when he sat down she left the door ajar and went out, saying:

'If he terrifies you, just call for me.'

'I will.' Sue actually laughed. 'But you're not going to terrify me, are you, Chief Crime Hater?'

'Not unless you're a very wicked woman,' replied Dawlish.

'Wicked enough to do what?'

'Be on one side and pretend to be on the other.'

Sue's voice rose. 'You mean you think I'm working with *those* devils?'

'There are such things as she-devils,' Dawlish said lightly. 'When did you first meet Sorio?'

She answered without hesitation: 'On Thursday morning.' Then, hardly drawing breath, she went on: 'Is he dead?'

Dawlish said quietly: 'He wasn't seen to come out, and unless there was a secret exit, then he died.'

She shivered.

'Just what happened, Sue?' asked Dawlish, gently.

She began to tell him . . .

And she went back to the beginning.

Sorio had telephoned her at her office on Thursday, the first day of the Open Tournament, and asked if she would let him go with her to the tennis. He was writing an article, he had explained, on the international aspects of the game, but didn't know Bournemouth well. She had asked him why he had called her and he had answered:

'I saw you when I was here last year at an Esperanto Congress, and I liked you.'

At that point she turned to Dawlish, and said simply: 'Such an approach is very flattering, you know. And he was charming, and really quite fun. He didn't know much about tennis but I was able to teach him – I do play quite a lot.' Dawlish saw animation back in her eyes. 'He was fascinated by you, Mr. Dawlish. So was I. So was everybody who didn't want Tony Haycock to win. You *were* superb, you know.'

'Nonsense,' Dawlish said, but he smiled. 'Did Sorio ask many questions about me?'

'He didn't stop. About you and, when I told him about the Crime Haters, about what you are trying to do. He seemed to think it was wonderful! So do I,' she declared.

'Sue,' Dawlish said, 'did Sorio seem more interested in the policeman than in the tennis player?'

'Oh, much more, but – well, I thought it was a genuine interest. He seemed to agree with me that most do-gooders are a dull lot, but you – you manage to make it fun.'

'How did you come to meet him at my press conference tonight?'

'Didn't I tell you? He was horrified – or I thought he was horrified – at the attacks made on you, and he wanted to find out more. So did I. I nearly beat my editor over the head to get permission to come to London. So we just came along. May I say something critical, Mr. Dawlish?'

'Yes.'

'The screening at the conference wasn't very good,' declared Sue. 'I expected someone to take out a gun and shoot you almost any minute. Getting upstairs to the taping for television and radio was impossible without the proper credentials, but downstairs anyone who had any old press card could have got in.'

Dawlish felt his heart sink, but replied jestingly:

'I shall have to sack my security chief.'

'You certainly should,' agreed Sue earnestly. 'Anyhow nothing happened, and I assumed you all knew what you were doing.' When he made no comment she went on: 'Then Sorio took me to dinner and on to the night club. I didn't really want to dance, but – I hated to say no.'

'Fond of him, Sue?' Dawlish asked.

'In a way.'

'What way?'

'I wasn't ever likely to fall in love with him,' she said. 'But he was so – so naive in some ways. And – oh, I suppose I shouldn't say it, he was so infatuated with me. I just couldn't bring myself to hurt him.'

'So he was in love with you,' remarked Dawlish.

'Mr. Dawlish,' Sue said, 'I'm not a babe-in-arms. I've had a host of boy-friends, some of them after everything they could get on the sex-is-fun basis, and some really in love. I do know what I'm talking about.' She was looking very straight at Dawlish. 'Yes. He was in love with me. He said it was love for the first time. And – I believed him.'

Gently, Dawlish said: 'I can understand that, Sue. Did it go any further?'

She shook her head.

'No. He behaved like a boy with his first love. Very proper. Very respectful. I liked Sorio, and in a way I was sorry for him.'

'Why sorry?'

'Because he was so vulnerable – and so easily impressed. *Too* easily. By me, you, Colonel Osgood—'

'Osgood?' exclaimed Dawlish.

'Yes – because of this work he does for the disabled servicemen's workshops – and he works himself to the bone for them, Mr. Dawlish. He's not only the president of the local association but of the South of England Association, and that's small beer with what he has done. He was president of the International Association of Rehabilitation Workshops a few years ago. Didn't you know?'

'I suppose I knew,' Dawlish admitted. 'But it went in one ear and out of the other. How did Sorio come to meet him?'

'That was originally why he was in Bournemouth,' explained Sue. 'He wanted to do an article on the International Association – to show how men who had once been bitter enemies would now work together for their common interest. Strangely enough they didn't get on very well. I think Ossy is getting very tired,' she added, and there was a note almost of affection in her voice.

'How long have you known him as Ossy?' asked Dawlish.

'For a long time,' Sue answered. 'I was once half-engaged to one of his grandsons! He' – those grey eyes had never been more direct as Sue went on – 'Ossy became very fond of me.'

'Then perhaps it wasn't so strange that Sorio and Ossy didn't get on too well,' Dawlish suggested.

'You mean Ossy was jealous?'

'If Sorio was so obviously in love with you, might not the signs of it have got on Ossy's nerves?'

'Well, yes,' Sue admitted, thoughtfully. 'I suppose so.' After a few moments her face brightened and her eyes took on a mischievous gleam. 'After all, I can't help it if I'm a *femme fatale*, can I?'

She leaned forward, and there was no way of knowing whether her posture was one of deliberate allure or not.

## CHAPTER THIRTEEN

## HUSSY?

SHE stayed like that, smiling, in as seductive a pose as a woman could show. Her eyes seemed to tease him. He wondered fleetingly what Felicity would think if she came in at that particular moment, but there was neither sign nor sound of Felicity. Very slowly, Dawlish sat more upright in his chair. It might be one way – and a very attractive one – to get Sue to talk, but it was not his.

He said woodenly: 'Did Sorio talk about himself?'

'No.'

'Not at all?'

'Not really.'

'That's no answer,' Dawlish said, sharply. 'What do you mean by "not really"?'

Very slowly and not at all put out, Sue replied: 'He said he had worked in several countries but didn't say which ones. He said he worked for the *Trumpet*, but never how he had become a journalist. He said the members of the staff spent about a year in each country, to perfect their knowledge of a language and then went on to another. He said they were not allowed to marry, but didn't say whether he had ever been married. He said that so much in England was different from what he had been told, and he liked it; but he never told me what he had been told against England.'

She stopped.

'That's all,' she stated with finality.

'I wonder if it is,' said Dawlish, in a matter-of-fact voice. 'No, I don't mean I think you're deliberately keeping something back, but you may have a lot of things tucked away in your mind which you've forgotten, and any trifle about Sorio might be of value. Will you stay here for a day or two, and talk to my wife, let her ask questions, and will you jot down anything that comes into your mind?'

Almost before he had finished, she nodded in agreement.

He laughed, 'Bless you! And, Sue—'

'Yes?'

'Did he say why he chose the Cloven Hoof?'

She hesitated before answering: 'I suppose he did, really. He said the trumpeter there was one of his favourites.'

'Had you been there before?'

'No.'

'Had he mentioned his liking for the trumpet before?'

'Yes,' Sue answered slowly. 'I think he associated it with the newspaper. He said the trumpet, properly played, was the purest sound in the world.'

After a long pause, Dawlish asked: 'Did he ever hear David Osgood play?'

'Yes,' answered Sue, quietly. 'He said David was almost as good as trumpeters in his own country.'

'And what country is that?' Dawlish asked, as if casually.

'I'm sure you won't believe me,' said Sue, her gaze very direct, 'but I don't know. He would never tell me. It's somewhere in the Far East, but where ...' She shrugged, and broke off.

He did believe her.

He was very close to believing all she had told him, but he had been fooled by attractive young women before, and there remained reservations. To make her understand this he said with great deliberation:

'Things would go very hard with you, Sue, if I ever discovered that you were the very wicked woman I talked about earlier.'

'You mean,' said Sue, full of mischief again, 'you couldn't bear to think you had been fooled by a woman! But be assured, Patrick Dawlish, I am always on the side of law and order. Besides,' she added, closing her eyes and leaning far back on her pillows, 'I want to avenge Sorio. I liked him. He was like a being from another world who didn't really understand this one and was always being pushed around.'

Her eyes stayed closed, and she did not open them again

86

until two things happened. The telephone bell rang in the main part of the flat, and Felicity came towards the room. Dawlish opened the door wide, whispered: 'Stay with her,' and went quickly to the nearest telephone extension. In his eagerness he knocked the receiver to one side. Regaining it, he heard a man's voice saying:

'Hallo, hallo. Mr. Dawlish, are you there? *Hallo!*'

'Yes, I'm here,' Dawlish said breathlessly. 'I knocked the telephone over. Who . . .?' Then he realized who this was, and said: 'Chumley – are you still with the prisoner?'

'I've traced him, sir,' Chumley the language expert replied with obvious satisfaction. 'He's a Shangrian, sir – from the island Shangri, off the coast of Burma in the Bay of Bengal.'

At once Dawlish saw a vivid mental picture of a map of India and Burma, with the vast Bay of Bengal in between. Here was one of the great hurricane and flood areas of the world, and also one of the most remote. There were hundreds of islands stretching as far south as the Andamans and the Nicobars. Many had virtually remained cut off from the world having neither economic nor military importance, but Shangri was one of the largest. Many believed that the fabled Shangri La had been named after it, for before the great wars, the great empires, the great trade routes, life on Shangri had been idyllic, and the polygamous people happy in a way unknown today.

Chumley went on: 'I've just done some checking. In the Shangrian archipelago, there are about fifteen million people, mostly farmers and fishermen. There's also a strong priesthood, not unlike Buddhists. The chap we caught is a trainee priest.'

'You mean he's talked?' Dawlish exclaimed.

'Once I got a man who can speak Shangri over here there wasn't much difficulty.' Chumley could not be blamed for sounding smug. 'And identifying him as a novitiate really did the trick. He says there are many hundreds in London, and thousands throughout the world – they're supposed to be acting as missionaries. Rather like the Seventh Day Adventists and the Mormons,' went on the knowledgeable Chumley. 'But that's as far as we got, sir. He won't say why he was at the Yard ready to kill you, except that he'd had his orders.'

'A fanatic,' Dawlish said almost to himself.

'Not much doubt about that, sir. And religious fanatics can give a lot more trouble than most. Any special instructions?'

'Did he have any badge or identification card on him?' asked Dawlish, telling himself he should have checked before.

'No, sir,' answered Chumley, 'but I'll tell you what was found near the spot where he was caught. A little lapel button in the shape of a trumpet. Gold or brass, I couldn't say which.'

'Have it checked for fingerprints,' ordered Dawlish. 'And keep him under lock and key. Make a written report as soon as you can and have the night staff make plenty of copies. I'll come over—'

There was a *ck-ck-ck* on the telephone, as if he were being cut off, and then a man said with brisk urgency: 'Sorry to interrupt you, sir, but there is an urgent call for you from Information. Can your other caller call back?'

'See you, Chumley, and nice work,' Dawlish said. He did not need to speak to the other again, for there were more *ck-ck-ck-ing* noises in his ear before a man asked brusquely:

'Is Mr. Dawlish there or isn't he?'

'Dawlish here,' Dawlish said.

'Ah – good news at last, sir. I've had a hell of a time getting through to you and I know you'll want this report at once. It's from the scene of the fire in Dean Street – the night club known as the Cloven Hoof.'

'Well?' Dawlish barked.

'Place was absolutely gutted, sir. The fire burned itself out quickly and some fire officers got right down to the night spot itself, to see if anyone else was alive, but the fire was so fierce the bodies have disintegrated. Band went up like the rest,' the caller went on, 'but there is one remarkable thing.' He paused, either for breath or for effect, and then went on: 'Every band instrument is intact. Even the cables for the electric guitars. Absolutely undamaged by the fire, although everything else is a charred mess.'

Dawlish stood very still.

He could picture the red glow and could almost 'feel' the heat from burning cars. Once these fires began they became infernos in a second, and almost nothing survived. Metal became twisted; flesh shrivelled; bones burned to ashes.

But the musical instruments had survived!

'Are you still there, sir?' asked the other man.

'Yes,' Dawlish said. 'Where are the instruments?'

'Here at the Yard, sir.'

'What department?'

'Fingerprints,' the man replied. 'I'm there now.'

'Ah, yes. Fingerprints. It will be fascinating to see if any of those survived on the instruments. Let me talk to whoever's in charge – by the way, what's your name?'

'Smith, sir. Detective Inspector Percival Smith.'

'You stand by,' Dawlish ordered and held on. After a moment a man with a gruff, old-sounding voice came on the line and Dawlish knew him instantly as a Fingerprints expert named Levy. 'Hallo, Levy,' he said. 'Do they still keep you on night duty?'

'It suits me better, sir,' Levy said. 'I sleep best by day.'

'Good. Have you had time to look at those musical instruments yet?'

'Not properly, but I don't expect much luck,' replied Levy. 'They've been burned clean.'

'When you're sure, send them with Smith to my office, will you?'

'Be there inside half an hour,' Levy promised.

'Good. Tell him I want him to have a car in front and a car behind his,' Dawlish said. 'Thanks.' He rang off. Thoughts were going through his mind like lightning flashes. At last, he moved towards the big room. Felicity was looking at the evening newspapers, and the sound of music from a record player stole gently about the flat. By her side were two glasses, and she picked one up and handed it to him.

'Thanks.' He drank. 'How is she?'

'Asleep,' answered Felicity.

'Not foxing?'

'No one foxes with the sedative I gave her,' replied Felicity.

Dawlish smiled faintly. 'Bless you. She was lucky to get out of that holocaust at all. Do you know what else survived?' When she made no attempt to reply, he laughed in a staccato way. 'No. You couldn't. The band instruments. Guitars, trumpets, saxophones.' He stretched out for a telephone.

'Deputy A.C.'s office.'

'Is Chief Inspector Chumley still there?' asked Dawlish.

'I *think* so, sir – hold on.' There was only a moment's pause before Chumley came on the line.

'Sir?'

'Our prisoner from Shangri,' Dawlish said. 'Did he say where he lives in London?'

'I couldn't get it out of him, sir.'

'Try again while I'm on my way over, will you?' Dawlish said. 'If someone happens to know the Shangrian for Trumpet House, try that on him.'

'Trumpet or Strumpet, sir?'

Dawlish wasn't sure whether that was a serious question or whether it was Chumley's idea of a joke, and he replied simply:

'No S.'

'Trumpet House, I've got it,' Chumley said.

'And have everything taken from the man's pockets available for me within the next half-hour, please.'

'I'll pass the instruction on,' Chumley promised.

'Thanks.' Dawlish lowered the receiver and Felicity took it from him. He lay back wearily. 'Sweetheart, I can't talk now because I can't yet see this affair except in little pieces of a puzzle, but I think it's taking shape.'

'I'm sure it is,' she said.

'Wake me in twenty minutes,' he murmured.

'Can't you snatch an hour?'

'Not this time. Twenty minutes . . .'

'All right,' she promised reluctantly; but she smiled down at him.

Felicity was quite sure that Patrick was asleep in a matter of seconds. Ever since she had known him he had had this facility to sleep for a very short period from sheer exhaustion, and to wake refreshed. He had acquired it during the war, she knew. She looked down on his strong, handsome face. Every feature, every line on the broad forehead, every hint of a wrinkle was as dear as it was familiar. His eyelashes were a shade darker than his eyebrows and hair, but corn-coloured described them all.

His head was heavy against her shoulder, but she did not stir. Her chief fear was that the telephone would ring, but twenty minutes passed without a sound. She placed her hand on his forehead, for a moment, and stroked gently: at once he opened his eyes.

'Time up?'

'Yes.'

'I don't know whether I'll be back tonight,' he said. 'I may have to catnap wherever I am. Don't worry if you hear nothing.' He sat up effortlessly, swung his legs off the couch, stretching to the limit of his great height. 'Go to bed,' he urged, 'and get all the rest you can. You know, don't you, that I could never do without you.'

The smile which accompanied the words and the words themselves made her heart lift.

A car was waiting; half a dozen policemen were watching; a car followed on the three-minute drive to New Scotland Yard. Many more policemen were in sight than when he had come here a few hours ago. He got out at the foot of the long flight of stone steps, and walked up briskly. He went past his own office and into a room a few doors along, which served both as waiting room and cells; there were three communicating rooms here, which could be used for a variety of purposes.

Chumley, the prisoner, and a stocky, black-haired man were in the room. On a table against the wall were the musical instruments – two guitars, two trumpets, two saxophones, a flute, a trombone.

'And here's a funny thing, a very funny thing,' Chumley said, almost as if Dawlish had been there all the time and knew what had preceded the comment. 'See, sir?'

'There.' The black-haired man pointed not at the instruments but at the plastic bag containing the contents of the prisoner's pockets. Outside the bag, dark against the pale colour of the wooden desk, was what looked like a miniature trumpet.

When he drew closer, Dawlish saw that this was in fact a key.

What else could it be but a key to Trumpet House?

## CHAPTER FOURTEEN

## TRUMPET HOUSE

DAWLISH picked the key up. A little descriptive tag dangled from it, giving the name and description of the man from whom it had been taken, the date and precise time, and a note about fingerprints. The 'name' was Shangri-l, probably as good a description as any.

'Has he talked any more?' asked Dawlish.

'The moment he saw the musical instruments he seemed to go to pieces,' Chumley told him.

'Dumbstruck.' Percival Smith appeared to be one of those men who always had to have the last word.

'Well, it doesn't make much difference,' Dawlish said. 'I think I know where this key fits.' If the words meant anything to Shangri-l the man concealed it very cleverly. 'Let's lock him up for the night.' He pressed a bell for some of his own men, who took the prisoner away, and then turned to the other two, saying warmly: 'Thanks, you've been a great help.'

'You mean I can go home?' Chumley marvelled; he looked as if he could drop to sleep on his feet.

'I'm off duty, if there's anything I can do, sir.' Smith was eager.

'No,' Dawlish said. He was troubled enough by working with Harris, a man whom he did not really know, and was determined to be absolutely sure of the calibre and character of everyone he used tonight. 'You've been a great help,' he repeated. He saw the disappointment in Smith's eyes as they went out. Holding the trumpet key, he went along to his own office, and called New Scotland Yard. The man on duty and in charge of the C.I.D. was Detective Superintendent Keller, an old acquaintance.

'Two things urgently,' Dawlish said without preamble. 'I'd like someone to come over and photograph these musical instruments – I don't want them off the premises just yet – and then I'd like the man in charge of the surveillance at Trumpet House in Kensington to be told to ignore me when I go there, unless I ask for help.'

'How will you ask for help?' Keller demanded.

'Probably by flashing a torch,' Dawlish said.

'Mr. Dawlish, you aren't going to take personal risks, are you?'

Dawlish hesitated, and then answered: 'No more than usual. Just ask them to be at the ready in case I need help.'

In a tone redolent with disapproval, Keller replied: 'Very good, sir.'

Dawlish smiled tight-lipped as he rang off, tossed the key up in the air and caught it, then dialled the number of the clinic; soon he was talking to the night sister, asking:

'Would it do Chief Inspector Pence any harm to wake him?'

'I don't think so, sir.'

'Then have me put through to his ward, please.'

Dawlish waited for only a few seconds before Pence spoke in the startled, over-loud voice of a man woken from sleep.

'Yes, Mr. Dawlish?'

'Inspector,' Dawlish said, deliberately formal and pausing long enough to allow Pence to become fully awake. 'I haven't checked your cross-index system yet but there's one thing you may be able to answer from memory.'

'I'll certainly try, sir.'

'In your inquiries did you ever come upon anything with a *motif* like the lapel badge we discussed earlier – a trumpet or a key shaped like a trumpet?' When Pence didn't answer immediately, Dawlish went on: 'Or anything to do with musical instruments?'

'Hold it, sir!' Pence was quite brusque. 'The trumpet – yes. After you'd mentioned it I also recalled seeing a similar *motif* on the car of the man Polkov, who tried to persuade Ryall to leave Astrid's. On the door panel, sir. I'm quite sure'.

Dawlish's heart began to thump.

'And musical instruments?' he made himself ask.

'Not – er – not exactly,' replied Pence.

With any other man, Dawlish would have demanded: 'Well, have you or haven't you?' But this man was thinking as he talked and in his mind there was some association of ideas. So he waited patiently, hearing the other's heavy breathing.

At last, Pence said: 'Night clubs, sir – that's what's on my mind. Night clubs and bands. Some of the missing research men were seen going to or at a night club. Some of the deals were settled at such places, I suspect. There was one in Birmingham near the Bull Ring. The thing which made it noticeable is that at least two of the men weren't night owls, if you follow me, but – well, they were footloose and fancy-free for once and you can never be sure what a man will do if he's off the hook for a night or two, can you?' Pence coughed suddenly, gasped for breath and then said in a husky, barely audible voice: 'Bloody throat. That's as far as I can go with trumpets and musical instruments, sir. Does it help?'

'It could help a great deal,' Dawlish assured him gratefully. 'I'll let you know more about this tomorrow.'

'If I could ask a favour, sir,' pleaded Pence, croaking now. 'Get me out of this place tomorrow if it's possible.'

'I'll do what I can,' promised Dawlish, and rang off.

He left a note for Scott, had a word with his own staff, and went out.

It was a long time since he had had so many men on his heels.

He was tempted to walk part of the way, but that would be absurd, so he sat next to the driver of his car and checked with Information about the exact position of Trumpet House. It was off Old Brompton Road, not far from the big museums, behind a group of houses in a small square. Once he knew this he leaned back and let everything go through his mind again – particularly the reason he was doing this particular job by himself.

He was going to use that trumpet key to get into Trumpet House, and he was going to search the house because he believed it might yield a vital secret. But he was not prepared to order anyone else to do it because it was possible that if the job were done carelessly, or even if something went wrong beyond anyone's control, there was a danger that there would be an explosion and with the explosion, a fire.

There might be a hundred arguments against it, but Dawlish was quite determined to take this risk by himself.

The driver slowed down outside a hotel opposite the big church of the Brompton Oratory, saying:

'This is the least noticeable place to drop you, sir.'

'Thanks,' Dawlish said.

He got out and looked at the lights of the hotel, then turned right and walked fifty or sixty yards. This took him to a wide turning with houses on either side, and halfway down on the left-hand side, he was assured, was Trumpet House. This was the only means of approach by road, although at the back of the house there was a high wall with a narrow gate, a short cut for anyone who wanted to go to Knightsbridge or Old Brompton Road.

He knew that the house was closely watched; that he was also under close surveillance from the police: but he did not see a sign of anyone. He must pass on congratulations. He turned towards the house which was in darkness except for a light in the front porch. The windows were all shuttered, and there was no movement in the grounds. These were about a quarter of an acre, a big plot in the heart of London.

The driveway was of gravel; on either side was lawn and shrubs. He stepped on the grass as soon as he could and approached the nearest corner of the house. There was a glow of light from nearby street lamps, it was surprising how easy it was to see: and to be seen.

Was he being watched from the house?

He saw no sign of life or light outside.

He reached the porch without, apparently, attracting attention. Three steps led up to it. He went to one side of these steps and mounted them.

The light from a single bulb inside a frosted glass shade shone straight down. A few moths fluttered against it. As far as possible he avoided the rays of light, though for that matter there could be no certainty that he had not passed through some electronic beam which had triggered off an alarm. A dozen men might be waiting for him.

He shivered as he reached the front doors.

These were double doors, with a brass handle on one, a brass letter-box on the other. Directly above the letter-box was a plate which read:

TRUMPET HOUSE
TRUMPET ENTERPRISES
THE GLOBAL TRUMPET

He took out the key and held it for a moment so that the trumpet part of the handle showed, and the serrated or cut edge of the blade, which did not look unlike the stops and buttons of a musician's trumpet, was concealed in his hand. He glanced at the keyhole, and saw that the key must be inserted with the serrated edge upwards.

He shivered again.

What the devil was the matter with him? Why should he feel on the point of losing his nerve? He actually wished he hadn't come, and winced when metal touched metal.

Nothing happened.

He pushed the key further in, until it was as far as it would go, and turned left – away from the door jamb. There was resistance but the key turned slowly. He pushed the door which opened easily, making only a faint creak of sound. He pushed wider. The porch light cast a segment of light into the doorway, and it also cast his own shadow before him.

There was no other light, and no sound came to him.

He stood to one side so as to get as much advantage from the porch light as possible, his eyes slowly becoming accustomed to the gloom. He could see a large desk, some show cases, music stands and musical instruments. Soon he could pick out the passages which led off on either side of the square hall. His footsteps squeaked: the floor seemed to be made of highly polished wood.

He fingered a trumpet which hung from a thong and a hook. It had the same feel as those instruments salvaged from the Cloven Hoof, and it was very light. He let it rest back against the wall; it made a dull sound, which gave him an idea; he flicked it with a fingernail but it gave off no ringing sound.

He moved towards the passage on the right, and as he reached it, a bright light came on above his head. He jumped back.

No one moved. No one spoke.

Dawlish could now see the staircase, and he realized that there was a gallery which ran round the hall. No one appeared to be watching, but who had put the light on?

He stepped back another two paces, and the light went out.

'I put it on when I stepped on that spot,' he murmured

to himself. He repeated the movement, bringing the light on again instantly. Did an alarm go on at the same time? There was no way of being sure.

He went up the stairs and looked about the gallery. The walls were lined with showcases of musical instruments, busts of composers mostly classical, though there was a copper statue group of the Beatles when at the height of their fame.

Passages led to various showrooms, and also to a long, low room the walls of which were covered with copies of the *Global Trumpet*. Offices leading off were marked: *Editor – United Kingdom* and *Translations*. Though small, these offices were up-to-date, there was a teletype machine, half a dozen typewriters; but nothing indicated an advertising department.

No one was in any of the rooms, and if there was a third floor no staircase or elevator led up to it from here. He went downstairs again, no longer startled when the light went out. One came on again at the entrance to the passage on the left which led to showrooms, a kitchen and some cloakrooms, but nothing habitable; the whole house was more like a museum than anything else; or the most exclusive showrooms he had ever been in.

He saw a sign: *Way Out*, and went towards it, reached a door and turned the handle. He had grown so accustomed to the weirdness now that he did not hesitate. He opened the door, expecting it to lead to the back garden, but instead it led to a flight of stone steps going downwards. There was a dull yellow light at the foot.

Now his heart began to thump again; but there was still no sound.

It was uncanny.

He hesitated, peering downwards, in a moment of indecision. This was the time to go back, call for help from the watching police, and explore with them the cellar and whatever lay beyond. The very silence made his decision for him, but before he went downstairs he checked the handle and keyhole.

The key was on the inside; in the shape of a trumpet.

He took this out and dropped it into his pocket and then began to walk down the stairs, keeping close to one wall. At the foot was a passage to the right. Lights were on everywhere, not bright but enough to see by.

He caught a whiff of something pungent: something *burning*. A flurry of alarm ran through him but died almost as soon as it came, for he recognized the odour: this was burning incense. Immediately he thought of Chumley and the Shangrian priest who was a prisoner. Next, he came upon an archway.

He heard men talking.

He heard chanting.

Then he saw the last thing he expected: a wheelchair, and some aluminium limbs; next to these a stack of basket work, and another of joinery. All of these were in a big room on the right. He went into this and saw that the artificial limbs had the maker's imprint on them.

He read: *Made by the British Branch of the International Association of Rehabilitation Workshops.*

This must be a storeroom below one of the branches of Colonel Osgood's organization; yet it reeked with incense and echoed to the chanting. He stood just inside the storeroom, out of sight of anyone who chanced by, tempted to go further in and to see how many priests were here, if priests they were. But he rejected the temptation: he had learned a great deal, and if he could get out without being seen, he would be in a very strong position to act. He moved back to the archway, and then saw three men walking towards it. He darted back to the storeroom, pressing himself against the wall.

Two were men who were not unlike Sorio; and he felt sure they were Shangrians.

The third man was Detective Sergeant Harris.

CHAPTER FIFTEEN

BETRAYER

HARRIS walked between the two men. His eyes looked over-bright and tired, and his hands at his sides were clenching and unclenching. But he was completely free.

They passed the doorway where Dawlish hid. A single glance would have betrayed him but they went past. Their footsteps made a strange tattoo, Harris's heavy, the others sharp and quick. Dawlish waited until he was sure they would have turned a corner and then followed, but he was still not certain whether to get out while he could or whether to find out more of what Harris was doing. He reached the furthest spot where he had yet penetrated, and heard a man say in precise English:

'Why have you come, Mr. Harris?'

Harris said: 'I thought you should know what's going on.'

'And what *is* going on?'

'The police found the band instruments in the club – undamaged after the fire.'

Silence followed: and then there came a hiss of sound, as if several men were listening, and had drawn in their breath at the same time. Then the first speaker asked in a taut voice:

'Are you quite sure of this?'

'I've seen the instruments,' declared Harris.

So instead of going straight home he had gone to the offices of the Crime Haters, must actually have known where to meet the two men who had brought him here, and come almost without time for thought; it would seem that betrayal was not new to him.

'I am glad to know this,' the first speaker declared.

'You had to know,' Harris replied.

'And I shall make good use of the information,' the other assured him. 'Thank you.'

That was dismissal, and Harris did not appear to resist or resent it. Dawlish moved back into the storeroom as the little party returned. Now he was in no two minds about what to do. He must get away. Even the temptation to see and so be able to recognize the speaker was only fleeting; he had tried his luck too far. He gave the Harris trio time to get back to Trumpet House, then peered out to make sure no one was watching, before going back the way he had come.

At every corner he feared trouble.

He met none; saw no one; left Trumpet House by the front door and returned across the drive and the grass, then into the street. No one appeared, there was still no sign of the watching police. He lengthened his stride across the square of pale houses. There was chill in the night air, and he drew it deep down into his lungs, in an endeavour to free them from the cloying odour of incense. Tension gradually eased from his mind and his body. He saw the lights of Knightsbridge and, across the road, the massive dark shape of the Victoria and Albert Museum. A few cars passed. Lights shone at the hotel and as he approached it his car slid forward. The driver opened the door.

'Glad to see you back, sir!' he said fervently.

'I can't pretend I'm sorry,' replied Dawlish, getting in beside him. 'Hand me that telephone, will you?' He called Information at the Yard and asked to speak to the man in charge of the surveillance of Trumpet House. Almost at once a man with a noticeable West Country burr in his voice spoke over the air.

'Chief Inspector Portallis, sir.'

'Nice job you're doing,' Dawlish commended. 'I wouldn't have known anyone was there.'

'We've twenty men watching that house,' Portallis assured him, and added with obvious pride: 'Not much that misses us, sir. I was very glad to see you come out again. May I ask if you found anything of importance?'

'Enough to help, I think,' answered Dawlish. 'Which way did the others go?'

After a pause, Portallis asked: 'What others?'

Dawlish was startled. 'The three men who came in after I was there and left before me.'

'I'm sorry, sir,' replied the man in charge of the surveillance at Trumpet House, 'but no one went in or out of that place except you.'

So there was a secret way, both in and out, and Harris had used it.

No one but he, Dawlish, knew about Harris's treachery, and the significance of that would become more apparent later; the most important thing now was that despite the twenty men watching, people could get in and out of Trumpet House at will.

'Are you still there, sir?' Portallis asked. The West Country burr was more noticeable in his voice, strengthened by anxiety. 'I assure you, sir, you were the only one.'

'Then there's an entrance we don't yet know about,' Dawlish told him. 'Don't worry about it now.'

'But it means I'm wasting my time!' exclaimed Portallis.

'I wouldn't put it as high as that yet,' said Dawlish. 'Just another piece of the puzzle. Good night.' He rang off on the other's 'Good night, sir' and had a feeling that Portallis probably thought that he, Dawlish, was having hallucinations. Dawlish put the receiver on its hook, and then said to the driver: 'Drive around for a bit, will you? I'd like to look at all the roads near the place I've been to. Do you know the area well?'

'Like the back of my hand,' the other assured him.

Five minutes later Dawlish passed the outside wall which surrounded Trumpet House, and saw the long, low building adjacent to it. Along the front in neon lighting were the words:

*Rehabilitation Workshops*
*London Headquarters*

'Go round the back of that building,' Dawlish ordered.

'The Disabled Workshops, sir?' The driver used the old name.

'Please.'

'Wonderful organization, that,' declared the driver.

'Yes,' Dawlish agreed, and drew a deep breath. 'And worldwide.'

'Can't help thinking that it's better in a way when these things stay at home,' remarked the driver. 'But I suppose it's like everything else. You have to get bigger and better or you get eaten up by the big boys. They make some wonderful things now, but I think there are a lot of cheap imports from Japan and Singapore and Hong Kong. Pity in a way, sir.'

'I see what you mean,' Dawlish replied.

Then he saw the small house at the far end of the workshops, outside the area the police were watching. He had little doubt that Harris had been taken in that way.

Twenty minutes later Dawlish hurried up the stone steps of New Scotland Yard, on his way to his office. No one was in. He looked into the C2 box and found a few more replies, none of them significant. Now he began to rough out

101

a message to send to all Crime Haters delegates. It wasn't easy, for he was tired, but he needed to get it on paper while everything was fresh in his mind. His first list read:

1. Musical instruments
2. Instantaneous combustion
3. Enemy within – H.
4. Toys?
5. Rehabilitation Trades and Workshops
6. Colonel Osgood?
7. Trumpet House. The *Trumpet*.
8. Shangrians – and incense
9. Importance to unknown Shangrian of news that the instruments had been recovered undamaged
10. Keys (Trumpet)
11. Lapel Badge (Trumpet)
12. Use of offices of 5 (above) as entrance to Trumpet House
13. Night clubs – and fact that some of the missing research workers had last been seen at one (out of character)
14. Night clubs – use of as meeting place to discuss offers to research workers
15. Night clubs not the *only* places where musical instruments used – check all bands, old and new (mod)
16. Sue Day – can she be trusted?

He stared at that last note for a moment, and then involuntarily shivered. If she couldn't be, then he was taking a wild chance with Felicity. His mind was so tired it seemed to be buzzing, and his eyes stung. He studied the list and added a few *aides memoires* such as *H.K.*, *Sing*. and *Japan* after *4. Toys?* and then pressed for a clerk from the next room. A middle-aged man came in.

'Hallo, Jackson,' Dawlish said. 'Can you get this typed with three or four carbon copies, at once?'

Jackson cast his grey eyes down the list.

'Won't take me more than five minutes,' he asserted.

'Good. Bring me two, one for myself, one for Mr. Scott in the morning, and keep the others on file. If I've fallen asleep when you get back, wake me.'

Jackson took him seriously. 'I will, sir.'

The five minutes seemed to grow into ten. Dawlish's eyes grew heavier and heavier, he could hardly keep them open. He started when the door opened and Jackson came in again with the two copies of the notes in his hands.

'Here we are, sir . . .'

Dawlish folded the papers, rechecked all messages, and went out again to the waiting chauffeur, who was by the side of the car. A cold wind was blowing off the Thames; and clouds covered the moon. Dawlish noticed that police were still outside the Houses of Parliament. More police were at the foyer of his building, and in the hallway outside his flat. Yet despite all this evidence of security his heart was beating fast with unbidden anxiety.

Everything in the flat appeared normal.

He made himself go along to the spare room and open the door. Sue Day was lying on her side, one arm over the bedclothes. She was wearing a hairnet, and he found himself grinning. He peeped into the main bedroom, and stood with his hand on the door.

Felicity lay facing him, the sheet drawn up so that only her face showed. She looked completely at peace. This was a very large room and against one wall was another bed of extra length in case either of them was restless. His dressing-room was next to the bathroom and he went across, stripped, and was half-in, half-out, of his pyjamas when a thought exploded in his mind.

'My God!' he breathed.

He streaked across the bedroom and into the big room, snatched up the receiver and dialled Sir Arthur Winthrop's number. It began to ring: *brrr-brrr; brrr-brrr*. He stood there, silently waiting, congratulating himself that the half of the pyjamas he was in, was the half he, in modesty, would have chosen, when the answering voice came to him.

'Winthrop,' it said gruffly.

'Dawlish,' said Dawlish. 'Sorry, sir. We need every orchestra, every band, big or small, London or provincial, raided for their instruments and for any Shangrian members at once. I'm not sure I'm not too late already, I've only just realized that it's necessary.'

Winthrop was silent only for seconds, but they seemed to drag on for minutes. At last, he said:

'Come and see me in the morning and tell me what's

happening. Meanwhile, I'll talk to Rice' – Rice was the Assistant Commissioner for Crime and technically Dawlish's senior – 'and tell him I've told you to get it started.'

Dawlish said fervently: 'Thank God for you, sir.' He rang off, hesitated, then dialled Information at the Yard. 'Who's in charge?' he asked.

'Superintendent Wiseman.'

'Put me through, please.'

'Right away, sir.'

Dawlish did not know Wiseman well. It was when dealing with senior men on the C.I.D. proper and in the Special Branch that he was at most disadvantage; he could not call on personal loyalties, and red tape could strangle.

'Mr. Dawlish?'

'Yes, Superintendent, I've a problem,' Dawlish said. 'I want to round up all the bands and orchestras in the country, and check their instruments and their members. Some may be dark-skinned – Shangrians. Do you know Shangri?'

'I was in the Burma campaign,' Wiseman answered.

'Good. It doesn't matter whether they play at night clubs or at the Albert Hall, we need to check them. And it will be some time – too long, probably – before authority—'

'Nothing to stop me sending a teletype out right away, sir,' Wiseman said calmly. 'I'm glad to take your instruction. London *and* the provinces?'

'In the quickest way you can. I – *my God!*' he breathed again.

'What's that, sir?' asked Wiseman.

'Have you ever had one of those days when you think of everything by deferred reaction?' asked Dawlish, and without giving the other man a chance to respond he went on: 'Will you add to that a watch on all known members of the Shangrian religious groups – particularly the one known as Shangri Lama.'

'You'd like to know where they meet and if they've any association with musical groups?'

Dawlish gulped.

'Yes,' he said. 'Exactly that. I was actually afraid you might be obstructive,' he added apologetically.

Wiseman said innocently: 'Obstructive, sir?' but he laughed. 'I'll get busy right away. Is there anything else?'

'Yes,' Dawlish said. 'I'd like all shops and offices of the

Disabled Workshops watched. It's possible some are being used by Shangrians.'

'I'll send the orders out,' promised Wiseman.

Dawlish rang off, with the broadest grin he had given for a long time. He dropped on to the couch with a gargantuan yawn, pushing a cushion into position for a pillow. In minutes, he was asleep.

<br>

CHAPTER SIXTEEN

## CONFLICT

In the heart of a small Midlands town, not far from Kenilworth, a couple who lived in at a small bar and night club slept restlessly on a divan on the first floor. The bar was on the ground floor, and the night spot in the cellar. The couple, a trumpeter and his wife, a little blonde vocalist, had come to bed late and were exhausted.

Neither of them heard the street door open.

No one saw the small, dark man who unlocked the door with a key and crept into the bar, then to the passage which led to the cellar. At the top of the stairs, he listened, hearing only the faint snoring of the sleeping trumpeter. Showing no expression he went down to the night club area and across to the bandstand. Here the instruments not taken away by the players were stacked tidily.

The intruder collected all of them he could safely carry, and crept upstairs with them. He placed them close to the front door and went down for a second load. Then he opened the street door and carried the instruments to his car which was just outside. He filled the boot and then the rear seat, and was about to take the driving wheel when two policemen appeared from a nearby doorway and a police car turned in at the end of the street.

'Hallo, mate,' one of the policemen said. 'Having a little moonlight flit?'

The thief stood petrified.

'Come on, mate, let's have a look at you,' the policeman said in his amiable way, and as he peered into the dark face he went on: 'You ought to be ashamed of yourself, bringing a bad name to your fellow immigrants. You're a Pakistani, aren't you?'

The small man gulped.

The second policeman was looking at the instruments. He whistled under his breath.

'Or are you one of these here priests I've heard about, a Shangrian?' asked the talkative policeman. Then his voice sharpened and he moved forward swiftly as the other thrust his right hand into his jacket pocket. 'Oh no you don't!' He caught the wrist in time and then put his own hand into the pocket and drew out what looked like a small, round cigarette lighter. 'Now what's this, when you're at home?' he asked, holding the cylinder very carefully.

A police car drew up, and a plain-clothes man climbed out, calling sharply:

'Careful with that! It could blow us all to smithereens!'

The small cylinder was in fact one of the self-timing explosive devices, one of one hundred and seventeen captured that night; with one hundred and seventeen arrests.

Not one of them exploded.

In the thousands of raids, only at seven places did the police get there after thieves had taken away certain of the musical instruments.

As the reports were sent into the Yard and analysed it became clear that the Shangrians had been sent to get the instruments at one hundred and twenty-four places in all, had succeeded in seven and failed in the rest. All the instruments found on the premises where men had been arrested were of the new alloy; and all had the trademark of the trumpet stamped on them.

Dawlish slept until half past nine, when Felicity woke him and gave him morning tea and the newspapers, half a dozen letters and four telephone messages. She stayed with him as he looked through them.

'The newspapers haven't anything new,' he decided, 'and the letters aren't important. Winthrop's called twice, Gordon Scott and *Harris*?'

106

'Yes,' answered Felicity. 'He wondered if you would call him at his home – he has a sprained ankle and can't get in this morning.'

'Harrumph!' grunted Dawlish, pouring out another cup of tea. 'I'll try Gordon first.' He sipped tea as he dialled, and was put through to Gordon Scott very quickly: a bright-sounding Gordon.

''Morning, sir!'

'And the top of the morning to you,' retorted Dawlish. 'What's making you so happy?'

'A complete success last night, sir,' declared Scott, and relayed the figures. 'Superintendent Wiseman called me just before he went off duty. I don't know what it's all about, sir, but congratulations.'

'Thanks. How many arrests?'

'Over a hundred, sir – in every band in which the alloy instruments were used there was at least one Shangrian member. And each of them had one of these time bombs.'

'Good. What about Harris?'

'Very satisfactory report, sir – including a commendation from Mr. Wiseman, as it happens. First-class reputation. People like him. He was seconded to us because he's known to be able to take the initiative and we like that in our branch. Nothing at all to worry about.'

'Ah,' said Dawlish. 'Good. I'll be in in about ... *What time is it?*' he whispered in an aside to Felicity.

'*Twenty to ten.*'

'Eleven o'clock unless I send a message.'

'Right, sir. Oh!' There was a pause. 'The total number of arrests is now one hundred and seventeen.'

'*Very* good,' Dawlish said, and Gordon Scott rang off.

Dawlish hesitated, grimaced when he sipped more tea and found that it was lukewarm, then said: 'Winthrop, next.' He dialled the Yard, for the commissioner would almost certainly be there by now.

'One moment, Mr. Dawlish,' said Winthrop's secretary, and almost at once Winthrop was on the line.

'What time can I expect you?' he asked.

'Will twelve noon be all right, sir?'

'If that's the best you can do it will have to be,' said Winthrop ungraciously. 'But I would like to know the connection between these musical instruments and these

Shangrian priests. In the beginning I thought you were investigating a wave of industrial sabotage. Orchestras, and Oriental priests are a long way from that, aren't they?'

'I wish I knew,' Dawlish replied.

'You mean you don't yet know what it's all about?'

'I know that all the one hundred and seventeen men arrested last night had these self-timing explosive devices,' Dawlish said. 'Also that there seems to be some mysterious connection between them and the missing research workers in the aeronautical industry. We also know the London headquarters. When I've been to my office this morning I may have more news – and I've a memo that must go out to the Crime Haters urgently.'

'Twelve noon,' said Winthrop, and rang off.

Dawlish had a shower and a shave whilst Felicity cooked breakfast; he was ready before her, and picked up the telephone, glancing at the number Harris had left with Felicity. The ringing sound had hardly started before there was a break, and Harris said:

'Harris here.'

'This is the deputy assistant commissioner,' Dawlish said formally. 'What is this about you being unable to report for duty this morning?'

'I'm sorry, sir,' Harris answered, 'but I've sprained my ankle badly enough to put me out of action. I wouldn't have worried you personally but something extremely important and confidential has turned up and I think you should know.'

'Why can't it be reported to Mr. Scott?' demanded Dawlish.

'It's difficult to explain over the telephone,' Harris said, 'but I do assure you it is of extreme importance. I hope you won't take the request as presumptuous, sir, but could you possibly come and see me?'

Dawlish did not speak at once. He thought he heard Harris breathing very heavily but it could be a noise on the line. Certainly the man waited, until Dawlish said:

'Not without having some idea why.'

'I do assure you, sir, it is extremely confidential and telephones have ears.'

'I am speaking from home.'

'With at least three extensions, sir,' Harris declared.

'Damnation, man, are you suggesting that someone here is unreliable?'

'It is very easy to tap or bug an extension,' Harris said stubbornly. 'I very much regret it if I am causing you offence—'

'You're coming damned near to it.'

'Then you must accept my apology. *My* line could also be tapped.'

'Now come on, man, come on,' said Dawlish irritably. 'Give me an idea what it is about and I'll consider the possibility of coming and discussing it.'

Harris said slowly: 'I daren't, sir. It's as simple as that.'

'Oh, to hell with you,' growled Dawlish, and he banged the receiver down.

In his apartment Harris said to a man with him:

'He'll call again. I'm sure he'll come.'

'I most certainly hope you are right,' the other said.

Dawlish sat down heavily.

Felicity had been keeping the bacon and eggs warm, and now, with the sigh of a cook whose masterpiece has suffered by needless delay, placed them before him. He ate slowly, then helped himself to coffee. When he went into the bedroom, Felicity was at her dressing-table.

She said lightly: 'You seem to be having one of your stern silent days. How worried are you?'

Dawlish shrugged.

'I don't know. I'm just – never sure I'm not putting my foot wrong. What did you gather when I was on the telephone?'

'That you don't trust Mr. Harris.'

'Hmm. Clever girl. What did you make of him yesterday?'

Felicity deliberated only for a moment before answering: 'Nervous, I think.'

'That would square,' Dawlish said. 'Is Sue awake?'

'No.'

'Find out if she knows Harris,' said Dawlish. 'Get her reaction to the wholesale arrests last night. Oh – and find out how much she really had to do with Ossy of Bournemouth, will you? She said one of his grandsons was dating her but when he took her home Ossy became jealous.'

'But what on earth could that have to do with ...' Felicity demanded, only to break off, and say in a low-pitched voice: 'Oh, my goodness!'

Dawlish pressed her arm.

'Never have to spell anything out for you, do I?' he said. 'Sweetheart, I don't know. But Ossy was one of Wingate's right-hand men in the Burma campaign during the war, and his job was to make sure the Japs didn't get any of the Hordaman islands. Presumably they included Shangri. I haven't had much to do with Ossy for years and I don't want official inquiries yet, but if you will talk ...'

'I'll make her talk,' Felicity said. 'Pat ...'

'Yes?'

'You do trust her, don't you?'

'Trust Sue? Not without reservations. But I *think* she's all right,' Dawlish went on more reassuringly. 'I must fly. I'll walk to the office and be there in twenty minutes.'

'What shall I tell this Harris if he calls again?'

'Where I am,' said Dawlish.

He stepped out to a cold morning with a spatter of rain in the air. At the entrance to New Scotland Yard were a dozen or so newspapermen and photographers, but he did not answer questions and did not pose. It was eleven o'clock almost to the minute when he stepped into the office. Gordon Scott was there with reports. A summary of the arrests confirmed what he had already told Dawlish, but there was a rider. Of the forty-seven rehabilitation workshops in the country all but one were exporting through the world organization to the Far East, and all but one had Shangrian liaison officers with the world organization.

'At some of them half the workers seem to be Shangrians,' said Scott.

'The tie-up between the trumpet, the bands and the workshops is becoming very clear,' Dawlish remarked. 'What else is there?'

Scott produced the latest replies from overseas, each providing more and more evidence of anxiety among aeronautical and motor-car research workers.

'And a new aspect is beginning to show, sir,' he said.

'The different corporations and countries are beginning to doubt whether any other country or corporation is filching these men,' Dawlish suggested.

'That's it, sir. Look – this is from Kurt von Strohm: "Investigations now make clear that none of the men most recently lost to our industries have been traced elsewhere." And then from Lance Severid of Los Angeles: "Suggest we all supply lists of recent industrial defectors and have all signatory countries check for these defectors." Which is virtually what we are doing,' Gordon Scott went on. 'No one on the English list of defectors, as he calls them, has been found anywhere overseas, so where do they go?'

'Very good question,' Dawlish said. 'How fast are you getting on?'

'Not fast at all, I'm afraid, sir.'

Dawlish said: 'Get me the matron at the clinic,' and looked through more of the reports. There seemed no doubt about the general direction of the findings: the missing men were not going to known corporations or State enterprises. He took the receiver from Scott and asked: 'Matron, this is Patrick Dawlish. How is Mr. Pence this morning?'

'Frankly, I don't think we'll be able to keep him here much longer, he is so restive,' the matron said with obvious disapproval. 'Perhaps if you—'

'Can he work?'

'It's probably what he needs, but if he uses his voice too much he might cause permanent injury to the neck muscles and vocal cords.'

'Let me talk to him, please,' Dawlish said. He pulled out the list he had prepared the night before, and had got halfway down it when Pence came on the line. 'Good morning, Inspector,' Dawlish said, briskly. 'I've a massive job in my office and you're just the man for it. It's analysing replies which are coming in from all over the world about men who have disappeared, but—'

'Let me come and get down to it,' pleaded Pence. 'This place is driving me mad.'

'*But*,' went on Dawlish, 'it is highly confidential work, and not a job which can be dropped once it's started. You would have to give the special undertakings needed and it would mean living in London.' He paused long enough for that to sink in, and wished he could see Pence's face when he realized what he, Dawlish, was driving at.

At last, Pence said quietly: 'I see what you mean, sir. I'm over the effect of losing my wife enough to be sure I would like to work for you. It will mean breaking my contract with Astrid's, though.'

'I'll talk to them,' Dawlish promised. 'Is a Yard man still with you?... All right, I'll tell him to bring you here right away. Good. I may not be here when you arrive, but my second-in-command will be, Chief Inspector Scott ... Goodbye.'

He rang off, aware of Scott looking at him intently. He paused long enough for the younger man to ask:

'These beggars have tried to kill him once, sir. Think they'll try again?'

## CHAPTER SEVENTEEN

## GREAT MAN


DAWLISH remembered that the attack on Pence had really been the beginning of this strange affair. He recalled the precautions he had taken to ensure that Pence wasn't attacked again. Was he being careless? Or now that so much had happened was Pence still in danger?

He said: 'Maintain a special watch, but I'm not too concerned. I doubt if he'll be out of the clinic inside an hour.'

'I'll get the watch checked right away,' said Scott. 'Come to think, no one has been told to slacken off with him, all we have to do is send an alert. Did I hear you say you might not be here?'

'I've to be with the commissioner by twelve noon,' Dawlish said. 'You know how to brief Pence, don't you?'

'Yes, sir.'

'If he really takes to the job you may have more time out of the office,' remarked Dawlish.

'The Lord be praised,' breathed Scott, and he looked so fervently hopeful that they both laughed.

A call came for Scott in the next office, and Dawlish re-read the list which he had made the night before. He added comments and questions, elaborating where he could so that all that had happened was reflected in the notes. He deleted the reference to Harris, against paragraph 3, and completely omitted paragraph 6. He sent for a clerk to get the list retyped, then picked up a pen and put on paper his doubts about Harris, and the reason, adding: 'I think I should go and see what he really wants.' Then he did the same about Osgood, adding: 'All evidence against him is circumstantial and no steps should be taken without a much closer investigation. Nevertheless he *is* the President of Rehabilitation Trades and Workshops, which appear to be used as a blind for the Shangrian activities; and he is very familiar with Burma, the Andaman Archipelago and nearby island groups.'

The typewritten lists came back in the form of a presentable report.

'Send that out to all international delegates,' he said, tucking two into his pocket.

'Right, sir,' Scott promised.

When he left, at a quarter to twelve, rain was falling heavily. For once he was glad not to be walking. This time he sat behind the driver, thinking of Harris, only of Harris. The rather slight man with Gordon Scott's colouring, the eager expression, the pale lips with their half-quiver of nervousness before he spoke; a half-quiver that was misleading for Harris wasn't nervous. It was his manner, perhaps deliberately cultivated. Certainly it had fooled Felicity. The thought of what he had seen and heard last night was uppermost in his mind.

On its evidence, Harris was a proven traitor.

Harris must then be under instructions to persuade him, Dawlish, to visit him at home. Who but someone who mattered would issue such instructions? The man to whom Harris had spoken last night for instance; to whom he had betrayed the discovery of the trumpets.

That hadn't turned out well for Harris and his associates, anyhow. Dawlish smiled drily as he saw the car pull up outside the Victoria Street entrance of New Scotland Yard. No one seemed to notice him, and this entrance was unattended; the main one being round the corner in Broadway. It was five to twelve. He went straight up to the fifth floor where Winthrop had his offices, and was approaching

113

the commissioner's private room when another door opened, and Winthrop's secretary appeared.

'Oh, Mr. Dawlish – the commissioner is so sorry but he will have to keep you waiting for fifteen or twenty minutes. Would you care to have some coffee while you're waiting?'

Dawlish hesitated, then decided that he would come back later. He smiled a trifle absent-mindedly and went back to the lift, which opened as he reached it. He went down to the fourth floor and then along to an office with the name *Detective Superintendent Sole* on the door. He tapped, and a very deep voice called: 'Come in.' He went in to see a man with his back to him sitting at a desk. Dawlish grinned, for the posterior overlapping the chair seat had to be seen to be believed! So did Sole's enormous shoulders, and roll of pink neck which lay over his collar.

'What is it?' growled the deep voice.

'A man with a problem,' Dawlish answered.

Sole pushed his swivel chair round from his desk.

'Good God!' he exclaimed. He began to make preparations to get up.

'Don't get up,' Dawlish said, moving to a nearby chair. He shook a surprisingly hard and leathery hand. 'I've only a few minutes, Jack, but this shouldn't take long.'

'What shouldn't?'

'What I'm going to ask you. Tell me, how good is Harris?' The brown eyes blinked between puffs of pale flesh.

'Want him for a special job?'

'Yes,' lied Dawlish.

'He might be very good indeed.' The expression now was bland and non-committal. 'On the other hand I suppose he could lack some quality you need. Here he was good.' The plump hands waved. 'Thorough, reliable, sometimes brilliant. Two weaknesses.'

'Ah,' said Dawlish.

'First, too clever. Just a leetle bit too clever. Managed to make one feel the job was easy and we all know it isn't. Tendency to make other chaps feel small – his manner, his upbringing – I don't know. I thought he might come a cropper here, but your chaps often work by themselves and you need chaps who will take chances.'

Dawlish smiled faintly.

'Fault Number 2?'

'Yes, but not quite so clear-cut as it seems. Harris has tried to do too many things on his own for us – I told you so in my report when he was assigned to you, but it's only one aspect of the weakness. He over-spends.'

Dawlish went very still.

'Mind you, he's said to have independent means. You don't need telling he's public school and Oxford, do you? But he over-spends and I wish he wouldn't. It makes him different from the others here, and . . .'

'Does he gamble?' demanded Dawlish.

'Don't we all?'

'Be level with me, Jack,' said Dawlish quietly.

'I am trying to be. Well, yes, I think he gambles with money, and with his job. He ought to be a freelance really. But good – oh he's good. Hope I haven't queered his pitch. Or yours,' added Sole hastily, 'or yours, Mr. Dawlish!'

'You've told me just what I needed to know,' Dawlish assured him. 'I must fly! We'll have a drink one day when the great ones are not breathing down my neck.'

It was twenty past twelve when he reached Winthrop's office again, and this time the great man called him in. This was a large, barely furnished office with big windows, a conference table at one end with room enough for eighteen chairs; Dawlish was usually here for a conference, seldom on a private visit.

Winthrop stood up and rounded his desk, to meet him. He was a tall, pale man who looked more ascetic than one would expect of a policeman, with a good crop of silvery hair. A chair was already placed in position for Dawlish.

'Well now – what is it all about?' demanded Winthrop.

Dawlish smiled faintly.

'May I put forward a presumption?'

At Winthrop's nod, he handed him the report, now already on its way to Crime Haters everywhere, and went on:

'Well, sir, I think a group of individuals, possibly Oriental, possibly religious-motivated, are trying to corner the world markets in aircraft and cars. Either cornering or killing, I don't yet know.' He explained the inquiries which were out and what Pence was about to start at; he outlined what had happened, and he went on: 'I'm not sure where these research workers go, I'm not positive what they're doing. I do

115

know they have a metal alloy and have made musical instruments, engines for motor-cars, pistols and time bombs
out of the stuff. As for the rest . . .' He shrugged.

'Was last night's the triumph it seemed to be?' asked
Winthrop.

'I think it probably was.'

'How near are you to finding out who is behind it?'

'I might be very close,' Dawlish said, 'and on the other
hand, I might be a hell of a long way off. The only way to
find out is to take a chance, and this I've decided to do.
And if I don't come back,' he added mildly, 'I suggest you
should make Gordon Scott the English delegate to the
Crime Haters and appoint ex-Chief Inspector Pence as the
man in charge of the office work.'

Both men sat still and silent, until Winthrop said: 'You're
quite sure the risk is worth it?'

Dawlish nodded.

'I don't think there's any other way of finding out quickly
what's going on.' He took an envelope from his pocket and
handed it across the desk. 'The usual after-my-death note
and all that. It will tell you where I've been and why.'

Winthrop simply looked at him.

'If you're sure this is the way to do it, I won't try to stop
you,' he said at last. 'Is there anything else?'

'No,' Dawlish said. 'Just thanks, that's all.' He pushed his
chair back and stood up. It was surprising how much
strength there was in Winthrop's grip.

Dawlish went out, into a drizzle.

He told the driver of his car not to follow; he wanted to
walk. He gave the same instruction to the two men prepared to keep him in sight. He walked for a few minutes
until sure no police were following, and then hailed a taxi;
soon he was outside the building on Millbank, and he
walked to the men on duty.

'When I leave, forget me,' he ordered.

'Yes, sir.'

He went down to the underground garage, where the old
Bentley stood beside Felicity's Morris 1100 and his own
second car: a Bristol. He tried the damaged door, which
opened and closed without difficulty, so the police garage
had lost no time putting it right. The engine turned sweetly,
and he drove out of the garage. He headed for Hampstead

but pulled off the road near a telephone kiosk, and dialled Harris's number.

The answer came at once.

Dawlish pressed the coin into the slot and spoke in the bluff voice with which Harris was now familiar.

'Harris, I am at a call-box,' he said, without self-announcement. 'I want to know what it is you feel is so secret. No more nonsense.'

There was a pause. It lasted a long time. Then Harris spoke.

'I'm afraid some of our staff can't be relied on, sir.'

'*My* staff?' roared Dawlish, as if this were an insult; but inwardly he felt a cold admiration for the nerve of the man.

'I only wish it weren't true, sir.'

'You can't possibly prove it,' Dawlish growled.

There was another pause before Harris spoke again, much more quickly, as if anxious to create a sense of despairing urgency.

'The literal truth, sir, is that I'm afraid to go to the office today because I think someone suspects what I know. If you could possibly come here, sir . . .'

'Where the devil *is* here?' demanded Dawlish.

'It's an apartment house in St. John's Wood,' answered Harris, still speaking very quickly. 'Apartment 40, Block C. Bonham Court. You can't miss it, sir – Bonham Court is off Bonham Road and immediately behind the Rehabilitation Trades and Workshops building. Block C is the third one along. Will you come, sir?'

'Oh, I suppose so,' Dawlish grumbled. 'Your story had better be good, though. I'll be there in about half an hour.'

'You won't regret it.' Now Harris seemed to be breathing heavily and with an effort. 'I'll be waiting, sir.'

Dawlish rang off, and looked out of the kiosk window. Not far off was an M.G., and at the wheel was a small, dark man looking over the top of an evening newspaper. Dawlish had no doubt that he was being closely watched. He strode to his car, and sat at the wheel, scowling ahead.

'He's coming,' Harris reported, and wiped the sweat from his forehead.

'He must come alone. You did not tell him to come alone.'

'He wouldn't want to be seen coming to see me privately, it would be beneath his dignity,' replied Harris.

'We shall soon be warned if he is followed,' the other man said ominously.

The first call came within five minutes. It said that Dawlish had not had time to make another telephone call, he had come out too soon. In another five minutes, word came that he was driving towards St. John's Wood, but was not being followed, and no police on the route appeared to take any interest in him. Immediately on this, came the news:

'He is turning into Bonham Court, sir.'

Harris, standing at a window, saw the Bentley turn from the main road and then slow down. Dawlish appeared to be bare-headed, and without a raincoat. He pulled into a parking place just within Harris's sight, climbed out of the car and approached Block C.

Dawlish noted that the building was seven storeys high. Shrubs grew close to the ground-floor windows, a few ramblers went as high as the second floor. It had a mellow appearance and was pleasantly attractive. The entrance was in the middle of the block, and the doors stood ajar.

He went in.

No one appeared. He saw the lift on the right and went towards it. Entering, he pressed the fourth-floor button. The lift went up slowly, but stopped at last. An indicator showed that Apartments 40 to 48 were to the right, 41 to 49 to the left. Dawlish turned right, and as he stood outside, taking a deep breath before he rang the bell, the door opened.

Ossy stood there.

Lieutenant Colonel Reginald Osgood, D.S.O., M.C. and bar, *Croix de Guerre*, decorations without number, stood there, leaning heavily on a stick yet upright and square-shouldered. He met Dawlish's eye without a tremor in his own.

## CHAPTER EIGHTEEN

# HALF-TRUTH

DAWLISH said: 'Hallo, Ossy. So you are the villain of the piece.' He smiled faintly and his voice was pitched on a low key. 'Am I to come in, or is this as far as you want me?'

Osgood moved aside. There was the tension of pain at his eyes and lips. Dawlish had the impression that this confrontation was a great ordeal for him; far greater than for Dawlish. From behind Osgood came one of the small, dark-skinned men, pushing a wheel-chair. Osgood lowered himself into it gradually.

Looking up at Dawlish, he said: 'I prayed you wouldn't come.'

'A twinge of conscience?' suggested Dawlish.

'Oh, my God,' Osgood said, 'what a fool you can be!' He was turned away in the chair, and it seemed to Dawlish that he bowed his head in an attitude of prayer.

They were in a small hall from which several doors led, and from one of them came the now familiar smell of incense. There was a movement at this door, and Harris appeared, half-smiling.

'I've been praying you would come, sir.'

Dawlish simply stared at him, and followed Osgood and the man who was pushing him into a pleasantly furnished room. At the far end, standing facing the doorway, was a man whom Dawlish felt sure was a Shangrian. He was grey-haired, and much older than any of the others he had seen. He waited for Osgood to be pushed nearer to him, and the wheels locked, and for Harris to draw level with Dawlish.

'Major Dawlish,' he said; and Dawlish knew he was the man he had heard but not seen last night.

'A wartime rank,' Dawlish said.

'Many remember you by it,' replied the other. 'I am Sa Di, the Chief Laman of Shangri, and the ruler of Shangri as well as the religious leader of Shangrians all over the world.' He paused long enough for that to sink in, then asked: 'Did you order the widespread raids on musical establishments last night?'

'Yes.'

'Then you have robbed me of one hundred and seventeen of my best young priests.'

'When you start a war, even a religious one,' Dawlish replied, 'you must expect some defeats as well as victories.' Vivid in his mind was the family scene at Bournemouth and Osgood's grandson's question: wasn't he fighting a different kind of war?

What kind of war *was* he fighting here?

'I wish to have those priests released,' the grey-haired Chief Laman stated, precisely.

'On what terms?' asked Dawlish.

'Their freedom for your life.'

'Oh,' said Dawlish, and actually seemed amused. 'It seems too easy, doesn't it, and perhaps it would be, if any one man had absolute power to say what would happen. Your men were arrested for a variety of crimes, sir. They will be charged in the normal process of the law and I suspect remanded in custody for eight days.'

'They must be released!'

'Pat,' Osgood said in a steady voice, 'he means it. Either you'll get them back for him, or he'll murder you. He will call it a sacrifice, but he will kill you. Don't make any mistake, he means it.'

'Oh, I'm sure he does,' Dawlish agreed, amiably. 'But the law's the law for all that. There is nothing at all I can do to release these men, priests or not.'

In the stillness which followed he waited, with those dark eyes on him, wondering if the man was forming a sentence of death in his mind. The features were quite perfect, the lips a delicate shape, as if they had been carved from soft stone.

Dawlish met the dark eyes.

'But other men could.'

The brows of the Chief Laman drew together as he spoke. He looked a sick man; pinched at lips and nostrils.

'You talk of others. What others?'

'A recommendation would go from Scotland Yard that these men be released for lack of evidence. Then they would not have to stand trial.'

The sick man looked away from him to Harris, and asked:
'Is what he says the truth?'

'Yes, Sa Di,' Harris said.

Sa Di, the Chief Laman; a name Dawlish would never
forget.

'Then it must be done,' Sa Di declared and his eyes
sparked as if with new life as he turned back to Dawlish.
'You can arrange this?'

'I could plead for it.'

'Then plead, at once! And if my brothers are not released
quickly then for each one a policeman will die, and if they
are prisoners for another day, for each day another policeman will die. You think I cannot do this thing. I can do
everything I say. Now go! Arrange . . .'

'Colonel Osgood,' Dawlish said quietly, 'I don't understand how well you know Sa Di and his countrymen, but
obviously he doesn't understand us at all.'

'What is it you say?' demanded Sa Di.

'I say that none of your brothers will be released under
threat, and I shall do nothing to have them released under
threat.'

'Then you will die!'

'Do you really think I care?' asked Dawlish softly.

He saw the bewilderment in the other man's eyes; yes,
Sa Di thought he cared. And he was right, perhaps he would
never know how much Dawlish cared; how sweet life was
to him. But in this confrontation he had one chance: to
make the man understand that killing and the threat of
killing would not get him what he wanted – but that another
method might.

Before Sa Di spoke, Dawlish went on:

'But there is a way.'

'You play with words.'

'I deal in facts. There must be a fair exchange.'

'What is it you want?'

'If your men were to be released they would have to return
to their own country.'

'They have work here.'

'They cannot stay and finish the work,' replied Dawlish.
'Nor can you.'

'They will stay and they will finish the work. It is the work
of peace.'

'They cannot finish any work if they are in prison,' Dawlish said. 'But if they were to be taken back to Shangri and work in their own country then it might be possible to release them.' In the tense silence which followed he went on: 'What work are they really doing, Sa Di?'

Osgood made a little choking noise deep in his throat. Harris's lips were puckered, and his hands were clenching and unclenching, just as they had been last night.

Then Sa Di said in a husky voice: 'I am destroying the weapons of war. I am destroying those people who have made a mockery of God. I am taking away from the great nations all those materials with which they make war. I am holding prisoner all of those who use their minds in the devil's work of creating new weapons, new machines. I am bringing back to the world the sanity destroyed by men of science. I have my priests in all the lands, making weapons which will destroy all known weapons. Here in England is the first difficulty I have faced and it must be overcome. It was by chance that the man Pence began to wonder what was happening; chance that he lived to tell you; that he lives at all. Chance—'

'Or fate,' Dawlish interrupted.

'It is chance!' Sa Di cried. 'And you will not be allowed to stand in the way. You will do what I tell you or you will die and the policemen will die, and one after another your great factories will be burned to ashes, and if it must be, the civilized world will be burned to nothing, and out of the ashes there will arise a new world, cleansed people, and—'

'It would be quicker by nuclear power,' Dawlish said.

'I tell you what is to be done!' cried Sa Di, his breath coming in harsh gasps; and suddenly he was taken by a fit of coughing that was painful to see.

At last he stopped, though still unable to speak. There was a blue tinge to his mouth and cheeks, which foretold imminent collapse. Swiftly an old Shangrian came in and hurried towards the stricken man, waving a small incense burner in an endeavour to help his breathing.

Dawlish, with cold deliberation, walked towards a telephone and dialled the private number of his office. 'For God's sake, Pat,' muttered Osgood, 'Sa Di means every word.' Two Shangrians approached on either side, but Dawlish ignored them. Over the wire came Hugo Pence's voice, clear and sharp.

'Deputy Assistant Commissioner's office.'

'This is Dawlish,' Dawlish said. 'I want two shots of adrenalin in disposable hypodermic syringes made available at the entrance to St. John's Wood Underground Station. It is extremely urgent for an asthmatic patient under severe spasms. The messenger must hand them to whoever comes up and asks for the packet, giving my name. Is that clear?'

'Understood, sir, but . . .' There was a momentary pause before Pence asked: 'Are you all right, sir?'

'I shall be if those shots come fast enough. Thanks.' Dawlish rang off and went back to the others, where Sa Di was still breathing with great difficulty.

'Pat,' Osgood said, 'it's all true.'

'And you are another of his priests?' Dawlish asked flatly.

'In a way,' Osgood admitted. 'Sorry, Pat. The situation has gone too far for me to back out. If only you had never interfered it would have been done without violence.'

'Except the burning of the Ryall family in Wilbury,' Dawlish said savagely. 'Except . . .' He caught his breath. 'So the research workers have been taken away and kept prisoner. Is that it?' He gasped inwardly at the enormity of the project. 'There must be tens of thousands! Where . . .' He broke off and looked away from Osgood, his heart as heavy as it could be. 'At the workshops?'

Osgood said: 'Yes.'

'But how could you persuade men of such intellectual capacity . . .' began Dawlish.

'They are drugged,' Osgood answered simply. 'The Shangrians grow a special kind of poppy which destroys the will power, and creates a kind of amnesia. The men are taken away and put through an intensive course of the drug. Then they are put to work all over the world, making small cars, time-bombs, guns, fire-proof weapons as well as artificial limbs and crutches. Thus they are removed from places where their brilliant minds were creating horror weapons, putting nation against nation . . .'

'Some might call guns and time-bombs horror weapons,' said Dawlish drily. 'But never mind. Don't you realize these men can also make weapons for peace? Better ploughs, better harvesters, safer fertilizers, anti-pollutants . . .'

'Do these things stop wars?' interrupted Osgood, huskily. 'I met Sa Di in the Burma campaign. He was even then preaching peace, he saw himself as another Gandhi, another great leader of non-violence. But no one would listen, and the wars went on. Do you know what made me join him?'

Dawlish said: 'Vietnam?'

'Not only Vietnam, but the senseless slaughter in the whole of Indo-China, and the revolutions in Africa and the piling up of armaments everywhere. The Great Powers talked peace and prepared for war. Weapons which would kill more and more people in one horrendous explosion, and – I couldn't stand it. I'd begun to hate it in Europe, when I saw what war did to the people of Burma and I hated it above every other emotion – patriotism, loyalty, courage, none of these mattered compared with my hatred of war.

'I worked for peace.

'God knows I tried. I worked with Bertrand Russell, I worked with the United Nations Association, I did everything I could to change the climate of man's thinking, but all the countries could ever think about were weapons of greater and greater destruction – until I hated them all!'

He sat, locked in that wheelchair. Every vestige of colour had drained from his face, even his lips were pale, but there was fire in his eyes and passion in his voice as he went on:

'I worked for the victims of war, of whatever nation.

'You may think my own injuries warped my judgement, but have you ever been with the real victims? Men without legs, hands, arms, feet, eyes, half-men somehow sparked with a will to live – needing help *which I had to beg for.*' He caught his breath and raised a clenched fist. 'Hundreds of millions of pounds spent on new weapons, on research for new ways of killing – and the Rehabilitation Trades and Workshops is a charity. People give their mite – their trifle. They run bridge parties and dances, organize marathon walks and tennis tournaments so that the workshops can just keep men and women alive.

'Do you wonder that I listened to Sa Di when I went to see him in Shangri?

'Do you wonder that I was prepared to do everything I could to help?

124

'He was prepared to act against the weapons of war – not against nations, not against people unless they stopped him. And he had discovered an alloy which would serve every purpose metal and plastic serve, something to replace steel and copper and the other metals. The manufacture does not cause pollution and the alloy is indestructible.

'He could make a new world, a world which would enable mankind to start afresh without the hideous destruction of a nuclear war, so yes – I helped him. I opened more and more workshops for him and his men. I found work for the research scientists whom he had taken away from the world of weapons and destruction. Yes, I helped him.

'And . . .' Osgood raised one hand and pointed it at Dawlish, and although his voice was calmer now, there still remained a quiver of passion in it as he went on: 'I will still help him. Even though you have forced it into the open and he has to use his fire weapon, I will help him. It is the only hope I see of making a new world. And he can start the destruction of mammoth factories whenever he wishes. He has only to send word to bands throughout the world to play a certain tune over the radio, and his priests will start the fires of purification. And don't try any heroics, Pat. He sends a nightly message. If none is received tonight, the fires will begin.'

Osgood stopped.

He was shivering, and sweat stood out in beads on his forehead and upper lip. He looked almost as sick a man as Sa Di, who still seemed sunk in a semi-coma, the breath rasping in and out of his lungs.

Dawlish felt as if he was in a trance. Horror was upon him.

There was no shadow of doubt that Osgood meant all he said with every fibre of his being. There was no doubt that he saw Sa Di as a prophet, the instrument by which all he believed in was to be brought about.

But Sa Di was sick and might be dying; and a message must go out tonight.

Dawlish fought off the trance-like feeling, and turned to Harris. His face was bleak and expressionless as he said:

'I don't know and don't much care whether you're a disciple of Sa Di or not. I want those adrenalin shots. Will they let you go and get them?'

125

'I'll get them,' Harris promised. 'Whether they'll let you inject Sa Di is another matter. Christian Scientists have nothing on these people for faith cures. And you won't frighten them by saying that he's dying. He's supposed to be immortal.'

## CHAPTER NINETEEN

# IMMORTAL

HARRIS had been gone for twenty minutes.

Little had happened in the room, but the incantations now sounded more and more like wailing, and the odour of the incense had grown stronger. Dawlish turned towards the window. Every movement he made was closely watched by at least three men and he knew that it would be folly to attempt to get out – yet.

But the nations had to be warned about the orchestral bands and their sinister tune, which would lead to the destruction of so much of the world.

He would wait for the moment – but he could not delay too long.

Harris turned into the drive, walking very quickly. He glanced up, indicating that he had the adrenalin. Dawlish turned away and stood in front of Osgood's chair.

'He's back, so we'll have to give Sa Di the injections soon.'

'Harris told you – they won't allow it.'

'Then he may die, and if he doesn't die, be seriously ill for a long time.'

'If so it will be the will of God,' Osgood said. 'Whether you and I believe that doesn't matter – Shangrians do.'

'What is going to happen to your precious new world then?' Dawlish demanded.

Osgood did not speak, but there was a change in his expression, a glint in his eyes, and slowly the truth began to dawn on Dawlish. Osgood saw himself as the Chief Laman's successor. Osgood saw himself carrying out everything the fanatic believed in. He might have doubts and fears, but he so hated the world he lived in that he would try.

Dawlish said slowly: 'You will never win the loyalty of the priests.'

'Won't I?' Osgood's words were tacit confirmation of what Dawlish both thought and implied. 'I've known them all for a long time. Next to Sa Di they trust me.'

Dawlish said: 'Trust *you*?'

'Pat,' Osgood said with a hint of savagery, 'don't push me too far.'

Dawlish shrugged and turned away, and on the same instant the door opened and Harris came in.

He held the package in his hand. As Dawlish took it he sprang into action, the only action he could take. He kicked aside the brake on Osgood's wheelchair, pushing it violently into the small gathering of men, then seizing Harris by the arm he flung him into the growing confusion.

Before it could be sorted out, Dawlish darted from the room, following the sounds of wailing and incantations. They led, as he expected, to a low divan, to which Sa Di had been taken, and where he was now lying gasping for breath; they had stripped him to the waist, and he had flung off the sheets. A bearded priest stood at his head, while on either side two others were kneeling. The sounds of their voices rose and fell, eerie and frightening.

All five of them reared back at sight of Dawlish, while shouts came from the room he had left. If any of the Shangrians followed him, what little chance he had would be gone; even if these five put up a fight he would not even be able to open the packet. Quickly he tore the wrapping off the boxed syringe, and then went down on one knee by the side of the sick man. His eyes were closed and he looked to be on the point of death.

The bearded priest uttered a shrill cry and lunged forward.

Dawlish thrust his left hand out, the fingers spread wide, and thrust the man backwards, then, with lightning speed, he took the sick man's wrist, held the arm straight and pressed the needle into the forearm.

The priest screamed.

One of the others struck at Dawlish but the blow was light, and he did not look round, but placed the arm back on the divan gently, and withdrew the needle. No one moved now; it was as if they all realized that there was nothing they could do. He put the empty syringe in his jacket pocket, and then stood up. As he did so, Harris appeared in the doorway.

'Did you get the shot home, sir?'

'Yes.'

'How long before you know whether it will work?'

'Minutes,' Dawlish answered. 'If it hasn't begun to take effect in five minutes then it isn't going to.' He watched the Chief Laman struggling for breath and, in those few seconds, thought that there was a slight easing. His own heart began to beat very fast.

Hoarsely, Harris said: 'It's working.'

Dawlish did not even take the trouble to nod, for the miracle had come with unbelievable suddenness. The heaving subsided, breathing was much softer, the wheezing was almost still. In a few seconds the Chief Laman looked as if he were asleep. His colour was better and his body quiet.

The bearded man stared at Dawlish.

The other four priests peered at him, unbelieving.

The incense curled and billowed about the room, the odour almost unbearable; but it did not matter now. He moved towards the door, Harris just behind him, seeing Osgood sitting in the wheelchair.

'He'll need at least an hour's rest,' Dawlish said. 'When he comes round he may be more ready to come to terms.'

'Why keep up that pretence?' demanded Osgood. 'He wouldn't be allowed to come to terms, and you know it. And even if he were . . .' The crippled man placed his hands on the control wheels of his chair and turned so that he could face Dawlish more squarely. 'And even if he were,' he repeated, '*I wouldn't be*. This has gone too far now. If you don't believe me, let me show you.'

Dawlish said quietly: 'The situation can still be saved.'

'Come and let me show you,' repeated Osgood. He gave a command in Shangrian to the other men, and two of them opened the door while a third pushed him on to the landing. But instead of taking him towards a lift they wheeled him towards another apartment, and almost at once that door was opened and he was wheeled through.

Dawlish followed, with Harris on his heels.

This was not a living apartment but a suite of offices, and the walls were painted with maps of the world, continent by continent and ocean by ocean. It was a political outline map, showing geographical features, and each city of any size was clearly marked. Some were indicated by one black dot, but by far the majority had a black and red.

'This is the Operations Room,' said Osgood, 'and I have an identical one in the cellar of my house at Bournemouth. Where there is a red dot we are in a position to take over or destroy all the big manufacturing plants very quickly. Key workers are with us and they need only the signal over the radio.

'Where there is only a black dot, we are not yet in control.'

He pointed to the outline of the British Isles, and except in Dublin and in Cork every city had a black dot only. The two in Eire had both black and red.

'We are as close as this,' declared Osgood. 'Do you think we will allow anyone or anything to stop us?' When Dawlish didn't answer, he actually laughed before going on: 'Nothing will or can stop us. If you try violence with me one of these men will kill you. You are as helpless now as when you came in. But you can change from a position of weakness to a position of great strength in a matter of minutes.'

'What do you mean?' demanded Dawlish.

'Have those one hundred and seventeen men released. Persuade Winthrop it was a mistake to arrest them. Then do what Harris has had the sense to do: join us. You could be invaluable in the new world, Pat. Accept defeat. Join us now.'

The man's very heart seemed to be in what he said.

Dawlish had heard such words a dozen, perhaps a hundred times: from men who believed that what he wanted most was life and power; men who did not believe that he could refuse the offer of them. 'Accept defeat,' Osgood urged, as a military enemy might urge an honoured or respected foe. 'Another kind of war,' his trumpet-playing grandson had said. Yes, it was all of that, and a deadly war. For every prisoner taken last night, a policeman's life, or else the life of two policemen.

Osgood really believed he, Dawlish, could be frightened into submission.

Dawlish said, as if wearily: 'It doesn't look as if I can do much else. But seeing is believing.'

'Seeing what?' demanded Osgood, sharply.

'The manufacture of the automatic time bombs,' Dawlish said.

'Oh, if that's all you want!' Osgood gave an order to the man at his chair, and he was turned round and pushed out, this time to the lift in the hall. They all went in, and Dawlish saw one of the men press the B button. Basement? They were down in a few seconds and stepped out into a wide passage which reminded him very much of the passages at Trumpet House. Some distance along there appeared to be a brick wall, but at a touch, this swung open.

They entered the workshop which Dawlish had already seen.

Here at least a hundred men were working at benches and lathes, with saws and drills, chisels and screwdrivers. Most of the metal was aluminium in colour, but there were huge stacks of a darker material: the alloy which Dawlish had seen so often.

None of the workers was disabled.

Some were making the small automatic pistols which Dawlish had seen; others were manufacturing the parts for the miniature motor-cycle engines. Some were making musical instruments, which stood in great piles. There was not much noise, mostly a droning of machinery which could not be seen.

'All of these weapons and the other secret things are made by men who on the surface would be making the horror weapons used by the nations,' Osgood declared. 'All the artificial limbs, the chairs, the surgical goods are made by the disabled upstairs.

'Now . . .' He paused. 'You wanted to see the automatic time bombs. Here they are! These two men are making them in sufficient quantities to supply all our likely needs in England, but reserve supplies are being made in other workshops. There is absolutely nothing you can do, you know, except join us or die.'

'I'm beginning to see what you mean,' conceded Dawlish. 'When can I talk to Sa Di? I think he'll be round by now.'

'The quicker the better,' Osgood replied. He gave a brief

130

smile of triumph. 'You see, I told you he would bow to the inevitable, Harris, didn't I?'

'You did, sir,' Harris answered. 'You did indeed.'

The big room upstairs was empty when they reached it. The windows had been opened and there was only a residual smell of the incense. The chanting had ceased. Osgood, still looking triumphant, wheeled himself out of the room, leaving Harris and Dawlish with the Shangrians, who seemed to miss no movement even if they could not understand.

'Mr. Deputy Assistant Commissioner,' Harris said. 'I'm sorry I tricked you.'

Dawlish looked at him bleakly.

'Are you?'

'Yes, sir. A hopeless situation had to be accepted.'

'Ah,' said Dawlish. 'Hopeless. What makes you think you could or should be judge?'

Before Harris could reply, while he was looking at Dawlish with the half-uneasy directness which was a curious part of his nature, Osgood came back, with Sa Di by his side.

Even Dawlish was astounded.

The Chief Laman now looked upright and square-shouldered. It seemed impossible that he could have been in such a prostrate condition only an hour ago. His eyes were clear and when he spoke his voice was strong and resonant.

'Mr. Dawlish, I understand you are ready to discuss terms,' he said.

'I've always been ready to discuss terms,' Dawlish answered. 'In return for your unconditional surrender, I will use all my influence to have your men released and returned with you to Shangri. I can't promise—'

'Dawlish!' cried Osgood. 'You gave me to understand you had accepted our terms!'

'I can't help what you chose to understand,' said Dawlish. 'These are the only terms I can discuss. Does the Chief Laman know that I saved his life?'

'I know. And I am grateful,' Sa Di said. 'However, the situation is unchanged.'

'The very things you say you will destroy are the things

that saved your life,' Dawlish said. 'The results of scientific research, new discoveries, new ways of feeding the hungry millions, healing the sick, helping the needy. Do you really want to destroy all of these things?'

'When the tree is sick the fruit is rotten,' Sa Di declared, somewhat illogically. 'I have little time, Mr. Dawlish. Your one hope is to arrange for the release of my priests.'

'Without whom you can't do your work,' Dawlish retorted. 'And your work couldn't be finished without you, Sa Di, and Colonel Osgood. One or the other is essential, or both of you together.' He smiled drily, noting the concern which appeared on their faces. 'You didn't really expect me to come here absolutely helpless, did you? Because I didn't. There are other high explosives which can do enormous harm, and there are also some of yours. In my pocket. If I am to die I may as well take you with me.' He took out one of the little cylinders which looked like a cigarette lighter, and went on: 'There may be a lot of trouble as a result, but without you two the consequences shouldn't be too bad. I left word that I suspected you, Ossy, and the workshops, and I also left word where I was going.'

He paused.

'It's a pity, but there it is.' He looked at Harris, his expression not without a touch of humour. 'Unless you can suggest a way out, Harris? You're not really with these fanatics, are you?'

'No, sir,' Harris said, smiling faintly. 'I don't know whether I'm glad or sorry that I didn't fool you. I've been trying to fool them for weeks, selling them information, but I'd never got to the Operations Room or learned what it was about. Will that thing in your hand really go off, sir?'

## CHAPTER TWENTY

## SPY COUNTER SPY

'OH yes,' Dawlish said into a deathly silence which followed Harris's words. 'It will go off all right, and take us with it. Ashes to ashes. Don't the Shangrians believe in cremation? Isn't fire cleansing?' Neither the old man in the chair nor the man who had been so near death and been brought to life again, made a movement or a sound. They stared now, at Harris; and there was amazement and disbelief in their eyes, but not venom. 'So. Spy counter spy.'

'I'm sure I can explain to your satisfaction, sir,' Harris said. 'But is this the right time?'

'No,' agreed Dawlish. He looked at Sa Di and went on in a level voice: 'The only hope for your priests is the unconditional surrender of everyone here. I'm going, now. So is Harris. If you try to stop us I shall blow the whole place up, and all of us with it.'

Sa Di's lips moved but no words came.

'Ossy,' Dawlish said, 'you obviously believe in what you've been trying to do. If you get a chance, *preach* it. Don't use violence to destroy violence, it only begets more.' He looked again into Sa Di's eyes and went on: 'I don't think you will be allowed back to Shangri. I think you and everyone who took part in the crimes will be tried and punished. But most of those arrested last night have committed no crime. If you really care for them, surrender now. Send them home to build a model country. When that's done you can start teaching the world.'

He backed towards the door, fully realizing that his chance of getting out alive was fairly slim. Now he held the time bomb at arm's length, as if about to drop it. Sa Di uttered no word. Harris opened the door, and both of them backed on to the landing. As Dawlish moved towards the lift there came the sharp report of a pistol shot.

Both knew that it was Colonel Osgood's way of accepting defeat.

The doors slid to behind them, and they began to descend.

'Go to the workshop,' said Dawlish quietly. 'The real one on ground level. Call Inspector Scott from there. Have this workshop raided at once and have all of the other workshops in England raided. Our missing scientists will be found at them.'

'You – you trust me to do this, sir?'

'If you don't do what I say,' Dawlish said, 'you won't have a chance of proving what you claimed upstairs.' He nodded and went towards the Bentley. When he reversed into the drive so that he was headed towards the main road, Harris was already disappearing. Dawlish watched the windows, still not absolutely sure that Sa Di and the Shangrians would let him go.

He looked round as he turned out of the drive; all the windows were blank. He drove to the Underground Station and called the office: again, Pence answered but Scott was soon on the line.

'Gordon,' Dawlish said, 'every band with a Shangrian trumpet player wants raiding and the Shangrian arrested. Worldwide,' he added, and explained enough for Gordon to promise at once to send out a general message.

So that was done.

When he headed for Central London he was sweating freely, and when he was halfway to Scotland Yard his collar was wringing wet. At Whitehall he hesitated; then he grunted and started off again, passing his own offices, and driving back to the Embankment. The usual number of men were there. He called to one of them. 'Maintain full precautions until you get fresh orders.'

Back at Whitehall he approached a police constable with a walkie-talkie.

'Can you get Information?'

'Yes, sir.'

'May I?' asked Dawlish, holding out his hand. When Information answered his call he said briskly: 'Can you put me on to the commissioner . . .?' In less than five seconds Winthrop was on the line.

'Dawlish?' he barked with anxiety.

'A lot to be cleared up, sir,' Dawlish said, 'but I think the real danger is over. You may care to read those letters now.

The one about Colonel Osgood is right, the other isn't. What time would you like me to come and see you?'

Winthrop said slowly: 'I'm not in a hurry tonight, Dawlish, I . . .' He broke off, and then said the last thing Dawlish expected. 'Where are you?'

'I'm going up to see my wife,' Dawlish replied.

'Why don't I join you there?' asked Winthrop. 'Six o'clock, say.'

'Just time for a drink,' Dawlish agreed warmly. 'Right, sir! And I can get everything else laid on by telephone. Including – are you still there, sir?'

'Yes.'

'Osgood has shot himself,' Dawlish said. 'The other man involved and the man who will have to stand trial is the religious leader of all Shangrians – the Chief Laman, Sa Di. I told him I thought that the men we arrested last night might be released and extradited quickly if he and some of his ringleaders will stand trial.'

'I will support that,' replied Winthrop. 'I'll talk to the public prosecutor and the A.C. at once.'

He rang off.

Dawlish handed the walkie-talkie back to the constable, and flashed a smile of thanks. One of the lifts had been kept open for him and he went upstairs, to find the door open and Felicity hurrying forward; so she had been forewarned and he was being thoroughly protected. She came to him, arms outstretched, without a word. Once inside, he hugged her until she gasped for breath, stood her away from him and asked:

'Sue?'

'She's gone back to Bournemouth,' Felicity told him. 'She said that now you obviously suspected Colonel Osgood there wasn't anything else for her to do. She has suspected for some time that he wasn't rational, that something strange was happening at the workshops. Was I right to let her go?'

At Dawlish's look of warm agreement, she went on:

'She thought your tennis was a pretence, and you'd really gone to see Osgood. You didn't, did you?'

'I did not, Doubting Felicity. But I expect Osgood thought I had, and when Pence came down, that seemed to clinch the matter.' After a moment's silence, he drew her into the kitchen and put on a kettle, and while they made tea, talked and talked.

Winthrop arrived at five past six, heard the whole story, and was in a position to cap it.

'The public prosecutor and the Legal Department are with us, Dawlish – those arrested men may be deported, but they won't be charged. Did you know that Sa Di and several of his priests at St. John's Wood are under arrest?'

'No, sir.'

'They are. The cellar has been entered, too. Sa Di made no difficulties. Once he accepted defeat he accepted it completely. The weapons are under guard. The kidnapped workers are under medical and psychiatric treatment, there seems some reason to suppose that once they are off the drug, they'll soon get back to normal. It's devoutly to be hoped,' Winthrop added, earnestly. 'You've had your overseas friends informed, I understand.'

'Yes, sir.'

'What I *don't* understand is the matter of Harris,' declared Winthrop. 'I can't pretend I'm happy about that aspect.'

'May I report later, sir?' asked Dawlish.

'By all means. But as soon as you can,' urged the commissioner. 'I know that your department uses some odd customers, but Harris might prove to be a bit too odd. Don't take too many chances.'

Dawlish almost snorted.

Winthrop left after a couple of drinks, and by then Dawlish was feeling much more himself. Well enough, in fact, to go to his office when he learned that Pence, Gordon Scott, and Harris, were still there. This time, he walked. He was followed, but had no sense of tension, only of sadness. He knew that the men on duty at the approach to the old Yard were looking at him with different expressions; the news was out, and perhaps the story of how the end had come. Two or three of the staff met him in corridors and in the lift.

'*Very* glad to see you, sir.'

'Good show, sir.'

'*Very* glad you got out unhurt, sir.'

His 'thank yous' floated behind him like echoes, until he reached his own door. After a moment's delay, it was opened. Scott and Pence faced him, the latter with his throat still heavily bandaged. Harris stood by the window, his attitude as always a little self-conscious and self-effacing.

Perhaps for once Harris was really nervous.

'Hallo, Pence,' Dawlish said. 'Making any progress?'

'Exactly the same situation in the United States, Australia and West Germany as here,' Pence croaked. 'By the time we've cross-checked and double-checked I think we'll have rooted out the Shangrians. The White House is going to extradite most of theirs, sir, or so we've been assured.'

'Home to the islands of Shangri, yes.' Dawlish moved to the window and stood with his back to it. 'Now,' he said. 'Gordon, you know this department as well as anybody. Hugo Pence will be on the inside, in charge of all control and records, you'll give him what help we need. Hugo – you can train others to stand-in for you. Two or three youngish men, preferably. I want Gordon freed for outside and overseas work as much as possible.'

'Understood, sir,' Pence bristled with satisfaction.

Dawlish concentrated on Harris. He noted that the man's hands were clenched tight and that his body had suddenly become like a piece of taut wire. Edward Harris; Ted, presumably. But not Ted yet, not for a long time.

'Harris,' he said, 'I ought not to send you back to the Yard with a recommendation that you be fired, or at best asked to resign. From the time you joined the Force you've been taught that team work counts. *Team* work. Now and again an individual stands out. He does some bloody silly or incredibly brave thing – which more often than not is fool-hardy – and then he's stuck with a reputation for being a loner.

'But this is a police force.

'It owes part of its allegiance to the Force here in London and part to the International Crime Convention or the Crime Haters. It's a team. You may think some members of it show off, or take unnecessary risks, and perhaps they do. But no member of this department takes risks which might lead to failure or disaster or to the death or wounding of his fellow officers without getting authority and without covering his flanks. Did you do this?'

Harris moistened his lips.

'No, sir.'

'What did you do?' demanded Dawlish.

'I – er – I'd been worried about the workshops for some time, sir,' Harris said. 'And the fact that they were doing so much business with the Far East and other countries overseas. I'd been watching Colonel Osgood for over a month. I didn't like what I saw, so I laid myself open to bribery. They knew I was on to them, and first offered to buy me off.' Harris paused but all he met was a stony silence. 'When I took a bribe, I was asked to report what else was being done against them, if anything, and when there was the trouble at Wilbury they stepped up the pressure. Wanted me to find out whether Mr. Pence had sent any information to the Yard or whether he was working on his own. I didn't know, and said so. They kept me so that if things came to a head they would have an informer at the Yard.'

'And what did you tell them?'

'Everything I could,' Harris said. 'That is, as soon as I knew it was on the way to being public knowledge. Finally, they wanted to see you. I – er – told them they hadn't a chance without you. And – well, I needn't go on, sir, need I?' Harris licked his dry lips and there was appeal in his eyes. 'I was armed, sir. I – I relied on you doing something that would turn the tables, but if you'd been pushed into a corner I *could* have got us out, sir.' He gulped. 'I could have got you out, anyhow.'

'No,' Dawlish said. 'At best, you think you could.' He looked fleetingly at the others and then back again at Harris. 'When I came this afternoon I left word where I was, whom I suspected, what I would do, what I knew so far. If I had died, the team could have carried on. If you'd died we'd simply have thought we'd had a traitor in the department. Do you see that?'

'I – yes, sir. Yes. I – can see I was wrong.' Harris muttered.

'Be wrong again like that and you'll be out of the Force like a bullet,' Dawlish declared. 'If I'm not here to tell you, Pence is. If he's not, someone will be standing-in for him. That clear?'

'Yes, sir. Thank you, sir.'

'Gordon,' Dawlish said, 'keep Harris with you while this job is being cleared up and on any others that come along unless I specifically say you're not to.'

'Right, sir!'

'Now, let's have a drink,' Dawlish invited.

Harris's expression was a strange mixture of gratitude, admiration and deep respect. Pence's showed open satisfaction. He said importantly:

'We've reports of wholesale arrests from forty-nine places out of the sixty-seven affected, sir. Not a single case of trouble. About the extraditions, now. Do you think we should attempt to co-ordinate them from here, or will that be better done at our African headquarters?'

Dawlish studied him, head on one side, then said thoughtfully: 'You'd better do it from here, but keep a close cross-check with Golana.'

'I'll certainly do that,' promised Pence fervently.

He did not seem to notice that Gordon Scott laughed and even Harris smiled.

THE END

## EXECUTIONER 19: DETROIT DEATHWATCH
BY Don Pendleton

Bolan wanted that fortress of Mafia power. He meant to level the joint, reduce it to rubble, show them what real warfare could be, get them running scared until they were falling all over each other and bringing their own individual houses down in the panic. He wanted to see shockwaves travelling the entire length of this Detroit-based empire, which stretched around the world in every direction, and into every country on the globe – an empire that controlled industries, international banks, multinational corporations, and even the policies of small nations. This Detroit mob was a festering sore in every vital organ of mankind.

So Bolan turned to Detroit with a determined sigh. Judgment had come to *Ville d'Etroit* – the City of the Strait...

0 552 10102 8          50p


## EXECUTIONER 20: NEW ORLEANS KNOCKOUT
BY Don Pendleton

Marco Vannaducci, the ageing local don in New Orleans, was dying slowly ... hounded by the feds. Marco was a desperate man, trying to hold together his tottering empire – an empire with annual revenues of around a cool billion. And a dozen powerful Mafia families up and down the country were waiting for the green light to get together and slice up the action ... Bolan had his timing right. He arrived in town for Mardi Gras ... when a combined invasion of New York and St. Louis mobs had also booked seats for the show. The underworld went beserk...

0 552 10179 6          60p

**PARADISE ROAD** BY DAVID SCOTT MILTON

Porter, Kitty and Eddie were celebrating Eddie's win in the boxing ring when they saw them first. Yolande, the woman was beautiful, with black hair and a pale face. Her husband, Matt Nathan, was tall, lean, and elegant, with soft sad eyes and a gentle manner. Angel Amato, their companion, was an ex-boxer – squat, with long dark hair and a punched-in nose. Matt seemed friendly, eager to put Eddie under contract – and as one of the owners of the Paradise Hotel, Porter reckoned he had the means to do so. Porter, that evening, had no way of knowing that this meeting with the Nathans and Amato was to have a shattering effect on all of them ...

0 552 10132 X        75p

**RUSSIAN ROULETTE** BY JAMES MITCHELL

Three highly efficient Russian exterminators were coming to London. Their target? Callan. The reason? He'd been sold out – by his own country ... his own section. But more than that, he'd been set up as a sitting duck for the K.G.B. He couldn't get a gun ... he couldn't get any money ... and he couldn't get a passport ...

For the first time in his life Callan was the hunted not the hunter – the victim not the executioner. And he didn't like it – not one little bit he didn't like it – and if those bloody Ivans thought he was going to make things easy for them, they had another think coming! He was going to fight – and he was going to fight the only way he knew how ... dirty ... very dirty ...

0 552 09762 4        60p

## YOU'VE GOT IT COMING BY JAMES HADLEY CHASE

'The world is made up of smart guys who get rich and suckers who stay poor. I've been a sucker too long: now, I'm going to be smart. I know where I can put my hands on three million bucks, so I'm going to take them.'

Hi-jack a plane and grab 3 million dollars in diamonds ... Harry Griffin liked the idea. Specially if it meant getting back at the airline that had sacked him.

Then there was Glorie. Harry was the ninth man in Glorie's life, and at her age she couldn't afford to lose him. So she fell in with the plan.

But Harry and Glorie were amateurs, they needed help: the only trouble was, they picked the wrong man ...

0 552 10138 9          60p


## THE THINGS MEN DO BY JAMES HADLEY CHASE

It was one of Harry's rules never to stop for hitch-hikers. But when he saw a pretty girl standing forlornly by her broken-down car, he decided to make an exception to his rule – an exception that was going to land him in a whole lot of trouble ... For the girl was Gloria Selby – rich and attractive, she had an uncanny talent for making money. And when she discovered Harry's business wasn't going too well, she presented him with a scheme to make him richer than he'd ever dreamed ... and despite all the dangers, all the risk involved, Harry decided to take her up on her offer ...

0 552 09934 1          45p

## THE DESTROYER: ACID ROCK

BY RICHARD SAPIR AND WARREN MURPHY

Vickie Stoner was a fully-fledged groupie. She was nineteen, red-headed, and worth one million dollars – *dead*! For Vickie was the key prosecution witness in a politically important trial and some-one, somewhere was willing to stake a fortune to prevent her testifying. CURE had orders to keep her alive ... not an easy mission – even for Remo Williams. And in the screaming chaos of the world's biggest rock festival ever, THE DESTROYER goes into action against the most expert assassins of the underworld ...

0 552 10017 X            40p


## THE DESTROYER: KILL OR CURE

BY RICHARD SAPIR AND WARREN MURPHY

A man had been found with an ice-pick in his brain; the state of Florida was in an uproar; and CURE itself was in danger of being destroyed. A stupid and dangerous security leak meant an un-welcome scandal in the highest government offices and threatened the very lives of everyone even remotely connected with CURE. Remo Williams had just one week to perform his own particular brand of miracle – one week before CURE and all its operatives would be quietly and permanently erased ...

0 552 10018 8            40p

# A SELECTED LIST OF
# CRIME STORIES FOR
# YOUR READING PLEASURE

*All these books are available at your bookshop or newsagent: or can be ordered direct from the publisher. Just tick the titles you want and fill in the form below.*

**CORGI BOOKS**, Cash Sales Department, P.O. Box 11, Falmouth, Cornwall.

Please send cheque or postal order, no currency.
U.K. send 19p for first book plus 9p per copy for each additional book ordered to a maximum charge of 73p to cover the cost of postage and packing.
B.F.P.O. and Eire allow 19p for first book plus 9p per copy for the next 6 books, thereafter 3p per book.
Overseas Customers: Please allow 20p for the first book and 10p per copy for each additional book.

NAME (Block letters) ........................................................

ADDRESS ........................................................

(SEPT 76) ........................................................

While every effort is made to keep prices low, it is sometimes necessary to increase prices at short notice. Corgi Books reserve the right to show new retail prices on covers which may differ from those previously advertised in the text or elsewhere.